MY DEAD HUSBAND

NJ MOSS

BLOODHOUND
— BOOKS —

www.bloodhoundbooks.com

Print ISBN 978-1-914614-65-1

ALSO BY NJ MOSS

All Your Fault

~

Her Final Victim

For Krystle, and for Mum x

1

'Your husband is dead. I'd think you'd have the decency to show some remorse.'

I held the phone to my ear, looking out the window at the sun rising over the sea. It glittered and, I thought as I let the news wash over me, it was quite beautiful this morning.

Kayden was gone: suicide, Paisley had told me. That abusive sadistic narcissist would be in the ground soon... and she expected me to be *sad*?

'Hello,' my mother-in-law snapped. 'Are you there?'

I cautioned myself not to allow my smile to come across in my tone. Kayden was evil. He'd sent stars of concussion glimmering across my vision countless times, had forced the sight of my own blood to become commonplace, had painted my body in deep purple and ice-blue bruises. But he was still her only child. 'Yes. I'm here. I'm trying to process it all.'

I had to leave for my bus, but it hardly seemed the best thing to say. I glanced down at the table where my half-eaten toast lay, next to the notebook I sometimes jotted ideas in. I'd sat down to this pre-work ritual with an estranged husband who refused to participate in divorce talk. Now I was free of him. It felt like a sharp studded collar being removed from my throat.

'He mentioned you in the note.' There was unmistakable vindictiveness in her voice. Her sweet Kayden could do no wrong. Shatter an orbital bone, snap a wrist: it was fair game as far as she was concerned. 'He said you drove him to it.'

The deranged urge to cheer whelmed up in me. I touched my face, as though Paisley had spirited down from Scotland and come to Weston, the small seaside town I called home: as though she was spying on me with binoculars and I had to hide my smile.

'Oh.'

'Oh? *Oh?* Didn't you hear me, Ellie? He slit his wrists and he said it was your fault. Surely that deserves more than an *oh*.'

I bit down a hundred angry sentiments. Confrontation – of others, of myself – had never been something I was good at. It either never happened or happened too passionately. Perhaps that was why it took me so long to leave Kayden. Perhaps that was why I was swept along by him in the first place.

'You've been kept out of the will and you're not welcome at the funeral.' Her thick Scottish brogue became grisly with rage. It was clear she'd expected something from me, some reaction, and I wasn't fulfilling my role. As if I wanted to be invited to the fucking funeral. 'You should be ashamed of yourself. My son was nothing but–'

I hung up.

It was easy, placing my phone atop my notebook, where it instantly started to vibrate as Paisley rang me back. She needed to rant and scream and take metaphoric chunks of flesh as her twisted son had taken real ones. But there were hundreds of miles separating us and Paisley wasn't the sort to drive down to England to make a point.

Her son had been nothing but a monster, a smiling demon

who raged and tormented the moment the doors closed. I refused to listen to her justifications.

I was free. For the first time in years, life was good, untinged by the presence of Kayden lurking behind every positive thing that happened to me. I didn't have to flinch every time a cupboard slammed, sure there was a fist soon to follow. *You didn't get the right pasta sauce...* I didn't have to freeze when a floorboard creaked at night, awaiting a hand slithering under the covers.

I didn't have to think, *Maybe he'll get bored. Maybe he'll go crazy. Maybe he'll come back and make me pay.* Because even after he'd left, that fear was always there, turning shadows into attackers.

With him gone, perhaps I could enjoy the good things, like my publishing deal. My book was going to be released in a few weeks and I hadn't allowed myself ten full minutes of happiness, because living with the aftershocks of Kayden made enjoying anything dangerous. Any second it could be snatched away.

'But he's dead,' I whispered, as though that would make it feel true.

And then I laughed, giggling as I hadn't since I was a girl: before I learned I was a little broken, a little strange, a little susceptible to the dark corners of the mind. I gripped my sides and I stared at the sea, revelling in the delight of my husband's death.

2

I walked out the front door with a skip in my step, far more cheerful than I'd felt in a long time. My ground-floor flat sat atop the tallest hill in Weston, giving me a view of the sea and snatches of the beach and the promenade. It truly was a beautiful day, the horizon glistening, the sort of thing it had been difficult to appreciate when I was constantly on alert for Kayden.

I headed down the hill toward the bus stop, fighting the crazed urge to whistle a tune.

My husband's dead, my husband's dead. I felt like screaming it at everybody I passed.

I sat down at the bus stop and let out a breath, warning myself to calm down. I was starting to feel ramped up, manic. I didn't like to toss labels at myself, but the truth was I'd experienced anxiety for much of my life – it was one of the reasons I'd never learned to drive – and anxiety's sister emotion was mania.

It was tempting to grin widely at strangers as they strolled by, to share the news which was making me want to shout in relief. I supposed that was better than panic attacks throttling me, but it was less than ideal. A man was dead. No matter who he was, no matter how revolting, it wasn't a reason to smile.

But that was bullshit.

Kayden had swept into my life as though he was *planning* on malforming me with his depraved designs.

We'd met at the beach when I was sitting down with a book one summer evening, my head buried in the pages, inhaling the scent of paper and sand. A shadow had fallen over me, and that should've been a warning: his shadow, the way he loomed. I should've taken note of that instead of his disarming smile and his silver hair.

He was older than me by more than a decade, but he held his age well, as though it was a choice and not a necessity. His hair was swept aside and his eyes were bright blue, stark, the sort of eyes that – I thought at the time – looked *into* me and liked what they saw.

'Nothing better than a good book on a sunny day.' His voice was thick and alluring and deep. It was husky. I hated thinking about how badly I'd ached for it the first time he spoke to me. 'Mind if I join you?'

I should have said no. I should have leapt up and lashed my nails at him like a feral cat, spat at him, done anything to warn him away. But instead I blushed and nodded. 'Sure.'

I was flattered by his attention, this handsome older man.

After that first meeting I was lost.

He did all the right things, made all the Hollywood gestures. There were flowers and dates and then, a few months into this whirlwind romance, he got down on one knee and told me how much he loved me. 'I never knew a man like me could feel this. I never knew these doors were inside of me. But you've opened up parts of me I never knew existed. Ellie Salter, will you marry me?'

Tears of unbridled happiness had flowed down my cheeks

and I jumped around in crazed joy. What a moron I'd been, allowing him to puppeteer me with such ease.

I glanced up when the bus pulled into the stop, jolting me from my recollections.

The past was often a pit for me, threatening to swallow me up. If I wasn't thinking about Kayden, I was thinking about Theo, the first boy who'd ever stolen my heart. But I couldn't think about my childhood sweetheart for too long without thinking about *the other thing*, the confusing thing I never liked to steer near to. It was too complicated, too messy, too terrifying not to understand my own mind and memory.

I climbed onto the bus and took a seat at the back, laying my forehead against the glass.

It hadn't taken long for Kayden to reveal the monster behind his smile.

It happened as soon as we'd said *I do*.

It was small things at first: the dishes weren't clean enough, I'd forgotten to straighten the curtains, his shoes weren't where he'd left them. From there it progressed with the everyday casualness of abuse.

How pathetically and tragically simple it had been: getting used to the way he would inflict punishment on me. A *thud* to the base of my spine, a stiff punch, or maybe a looping wood-thick arm around my throat as he squeezed and loosened, squeezed and loosened his grip over and over, laughing in my ear as my legs weakened and my world became hazy with how close to unconsciousness I was.

No, I refused to think about that. I'd picture him slumped with his wrists slit open instead, blood soaking into the carpet, his lips twisted into a deathly grimace instead of his usual deceiving smile.

That prompted *my* lips to twitch upward again, another grin trying to take hold of my face.

I took out my mobile, navigating to Facebook. I spent the rest of the journey responding to comments, liking book-related statuses, generally building up my presence amongst readers so they'd recognise my name when my book came out. That was how it had started anyway, but now I really enjoyed the interactions, the flurry of notifications and replies and banter. It was a welcome distraction from the madness of this morning.

My book was being published by a small digital-first publisher, meaning they specialised in e-books. That was why I felt compelled to do my part to get my name out there. In the indie spirit, we were all in this together.

I found myself able to view my publishing contract with fresh appreciation this morning. Previously, I'd let negative thoughts seep into my mind: *it's not a big publisher, hardly anybody will read your book, you're nothing special.* But now that Kayden was gone, I was able to push all of that aside.

I'd written a book. I'd edited a book. And it had found a home.

Perhaps those negative thoughts had been Kayden, whispering to me over the miles, picking at every little thing like he always did. Knowing he'd bled out – knowing he'd never bend me over the kitchen divider and roughly take me again – I let my head fall back, a feeling of pride moving through me. Or at least a cousin of pride, a convincing pretender. But anything was better than the numbness I'd felt before this.

I *should* be proud. I'd achieved what so many people strived for, a book deal with a reputable publisher, digital-first or not.

After sorting my social media stuff, I watched Weston drift by, wondering how Mum would react to the news of Kayden's death.

3

I rounded the corner that led toward Mum's house. I always thought of it as her house, though I had lived there for my whole childhood. The moment I'd left home Mum had renovated, as though she'd needed to put that period of her life behind her. She'd repainted the stucco exterior salmon-pink, added hanging baskets, tall hedges that framed a gravel path, flower beds, ivy creepers... and on and on, wiping away any sign of what it had once been.

I couldn't blame her.

We'd lived there when Dad died. His death had triggered her psychosis, her schizophrenia exploding back into her personality when it had lain dormant for so long. I didn't understand why she hadn't moved, but perhaps she thought she could reclaim the piece of herself that had died with Dad.

We rarely talked about such things.

This was the house she'd fled one evening when I was thirteen, a bread knife in her hand, utterly naked, a fierce glint in her eyes as she stood at the end of the pathway. There had been no hedges to protect her modesty then.

'I have to find them, Ellie,' she'd said as I stood at the door, pleading with her to come inside.

'Find who?'

'They're watching me. They're watching *us*.'

It had been an early Saturday morning and the street was waking up, music playing lightly from a window, a dog yapping a few houses over. Mum had flinched at every noise, her breasts bobbing offensively, making me want to look away even as I crept over to her. She'd gone through a phase of tearing her clothes off, convinced they were causing her pain. I'd learned by then to move slowly, hands raised, palms flat, to show her I didn't mean any harm.

She cried when I brought her inside and wrapped a blanket around her. 'I'm sorry. I don't know how it happened. I don't know what's wrong with me.'

I'd managed to stay calm through that incident, but that wasn't always the case.

There had been times when I'd screamed at her: 'Mad bitch, what the fuck is wrong with you? I wish I had a normal mum. I wish you were dead.' She'd shaved her hair off soon after one argument, convinced there were small electronic devices crawling over her scalp.

'They're sneaking into my brain.'

She'd scratched her scalp raw, scratched so hard her fingernails had blunted against her skull, convinced she would have to tear her head to pieces to get at the invaders.

Once, she'd erected an elaborate blanket fortress in my bedroom, wrapping tight knots around my bedposts, the door handle, billowing from the ceiling until the entire room was a criss-crossing interplay of light, changing colour depending on which blanket it was passing through. Perhaps this would've been fun when I was five or six, but I was a teenager and she was ranting the whole time, something about how the blankets protected us from the radiation, and they were out to get us. It was always that.

They're out to get us.

There were so many *theys* I stopped counting.

These sorts of incidents had become routine in the years after Dad's death. It was like the cancer had eaten away at her sanity as much as his lungs. But she was never abusive. Perhaps she was mean sometimes. Perhaps she allowed moods and imagined whispers to make her vindictive for a short while. But I always knew, when it mattered, she loved me.

The one thing that soothed her was when I tapped away at the old typewriter. She'd drag it into my bedroom and sit me down in front of it, a rare flurry of excitement buzzing around her, clapping her hands together as she settled cross-legged on the floor. 'Type, Ellie.'

'Type what?'

'Just type.'

And I had.

I'd typed, and somewhere along the way the typing had become as vital to me as it was to Mum. There was a beautiful freedom in words, as though the page was a window and I was peering into a different world. The room fell away, Mum's stench – she rarely washed – drifted into the distance, and there was only the character, the scene, the other world. It intoxicated me.

Later I switched the clunky old typewriter for a word processor and started to take it seriously. Mum had sometimes said she wanted to be a writer, but apparently she'd tried and it had turned her mad. She would never explain what she meant, and Lottie Salter rarely budged on something once she made her mind up.

As I pushed open the gate, glancing at the house, a flashing vignette of Theo passed across my vision. I saw him standing under my window with a wicked grin on his face, his mop of red hair in curly ringlets around his cheeks, waving a joint around before taking a long drag. I remembered how he'd taunted me with it, pleading with me to sneak out and go on an adventure with him.

But no... I couldn't allow myself to think of Theo.

It was a silly childhood romance, nothing else. And that other thing, that whole mess, it wasn't my concern.

Just as the mother from my childhood wasn't my concern.

Once *the thing* happened – whatever the hell it was – Mum had had no choice but to rise from her psychosis. I wasn't sure how it had happened, because there was something wrong with my mind, some defective piece I never pondered for too long. But she had arisen, gotten the right therapy, the right medication, and today Charlotte Salter was–

'Eleanor.' Mum smiled radiantly at me as she opened the door. She stood in her cargo trousers, her thick boots, her long-sleeved flannel shirt. She was fit for her age, her grey hair tied back with a violet bandana. She held her favourite watering can. 'Why are you looking at me like that?'

'Like what?'

She tilted her head, a playful expression dancing across her face. 'Like you've won the lottery.'

I laughed and danced over to her. 'I'd rather beg my dear old mummy for her last few pennies, to be honest.'

She waved a bothered hand. 'This again. You're welcome to whatever you need.'

I prodded her, revelling in her awkwardness. I loved teasing her about this.

Her parents – my grandparents – had been very wealthy, my grandfather leaving my mother a queen's ransom in his will. She was always telling me I didn't have to work if I chose not to, but I couldn't stand the idea of relying upon her, because what if she changed as she had before, and I was left with nothing... but these were cruel thoughts.

Mum had been sane for one and a half decades, or as sane as a schizophrenic woman can be.

She placed her hand on my shoulder, squeezing it tightly as she often did, as though she could make up for past coldness with present warmth. And she could. To some degree, she really could. 'What is it, Ellie?'

'Mum, he's dead. Kayden's dead. He killed himself. He slit his wrists.' I couldn't help it. I let out a giggle, the sort of crazed sound she'd made countless times when I was a girl. 'That piece of shit is rotting in hell.'

I expected her to clasp my shoulder tighter, for her face to crease into a smile. But instead, she took a step back. She scowled. 'A man's dead, and you're *laughing?* What sort of daughter did I raise? What the fuck is wrong with you?'

4

I stared at her, stunned for a moment. *Raised me, fucking raised me? I raised myself, you psychotic bitch.* I'd scream at her now: scream and surge forward, throwing a thousand things in her face, things we were supposed to have put behind us. I'd tell her she was a terrible mother for making me feel small about this, for stealing this moment from me. But that was the old Ellie and Lottie, before we reconnected and made amends.

I forced calmness into my voice. 'Maybe I shouldn't have smiled. But you can't deny this is good news.'

Her eyes flitted over me. I thought she was going to collapse into tears, her cheeks trembling.

Kayden was a monster. His death should've prompted cheering, not this nonsense.

Finally she nodded. 'Of course I understand that. Kayden, he was... what he did to you, it was evil. I hated him. But I simply don't believe death is something to laugh about.'

There must've been more to this, because she'd exploded at me as she hadn't in years. She'd made a point *not* to so she could make up for past instances. It didn't make sense. Kayden and my mother had only met a handful of times. He'd flatly refused to make an effort with my friends and family. When they *did* meet, of course he reverted to the old Kayden, the charming rogue.

Why did she care?

I'd since told her the truth about my marriage. She knew the perfect son-in-law was a lie. She knew in broad strokes of bruise-yellow and blood-red what he'd done to me. She knew he'd forced himself on me many, many times. She knew he'd used my belly as a punching bag and my legs as a canvas, only he painted with lit matches.

'You have to think,' she went on in a rush, 'if you let other people see you react like this, you could come across as the one in the wrong. People are strange where marriage is concerned. Even when it's abusive, they expect the spouse to show some remorse, or at least some seriousness. Or at the *very* least they don't expect laughter. I only have your best interests at heart, Ellie. But I'm sorry. I shouldn't have flown off the handle.'

'Maybe I shouldn't have laughed.' I didn't mean this. I'd rather be dancing on Kayden's grave, not that I'd ever visit it. I'd rather squat down and piss into the dirt and say the vicious things to him in death he'd said to me in life. 'Maybe we should go inside?'

'Yes, fine. Let me see to the plants, and then I'll join you in the garden.'

'I'll make us some tea.'

'Yes, I'm sure that'll be fine.'

I walked into the house, forcing away the memories which tried to grab me. They didn't come from the decoration of the house – Mum had paid to have everything modernised, sleek, almost clinical – but from the structure itself.

I remembered how I'd once kicked this wall after an argument, how Mum had stumbled drunkenly down the stairs and I'd just about caught her before she cracked her head, how she'd crouched at this window peering over the sill, hissing at me to get down, they could see us. They could always see us, whoever *they* were.

But there was no *they*, only an unfair illness and a girl too young to understand how to deal with it. But I'd done my best, supported her in every way I knew how. And what was her response, to *shout* at me when my abusive husband did the world a favour and took his own life?

Stifling a whirring of rage in my belly, I made the tea and carried the mugs out to the back garden, which was far more extravagant than the front. Long rows of vegetables sat in the middle, with countless potted plants at the edges, tactically placed between the flourishing bushes and lattices, a whole vibrant world.

'Are you going to attend the funeral?' Mum blew on her tea. 'Or would that be too much?'

She'd returned to her regular non-judgemental self. I decided to let it slide, as we'd both learnt to do over the years. It was better than dwelling on every disagreement. Neither of us liked to drag things out, to argue, to hold grudges, which was probably why our arguments were chaos when we finally exploded. Chaos and calm, an endless cycle. I'd never claim it was healthy.

'No. Paisley said I wasn't welcome, as if I'd want to go. The woman is deranged. She has no idea how twisted her son is. Was.'

'Parents always have a blind spot. I'm sure he didn't behave the same around her as he did around you.'

'But I told her. When we separated and Kayden went running back home. I got drunk one night, filled with Dutch courage. I rang her. And I told her the things he'd done to me. She refused to believe any of it.'

Mum reached over and touched my hand. My nails were

going *tap-tap-tap* against the mug from trembling, as jagged vignettes stabbed into my mind.

I saw Kayden looming over me, a dripping tool in his hand. It had been a wooden spoon from the sink, and the dripping had been water, but in my memory it became blood. *'Do you think I deserve to live in a pigsty, you lazy slut?'* And then it had happened, as it always happened, little pieces of my dignity stolen with each strike.

'I'm fine.' I placed my hands in my lap, picking at my fingernails. 'Mum, apparently he mentioned me in his suicide note. He said it was my fault because I separated from him. How deluded can he be?'

She didn't offer me the support I longed for. She nodded half-heartedly and sighed. 'People can be very delusional.'

I wasn't talking about *people*. I was talking about Paisley fucking Hunter and her son who could do no wrong. But clearly Mum wasn't going to give me the support I craved.

'Anyway,' Mum said, 'let's talk about happier things. Tell me about your book. You must be ever so excited. I can't wait to read it. I can't wait for the *world* to read it. I was thinking earlier about that time I saw you in the library, hunched over your books, oblivious to the world around you. You didn't notice me walk up to you until I was standing right there.'

'I was trying to read about mad Victorian women, and then a mad modern woman interrupted me. It was very rude.'

She laughed. 'Yes, that's me. Mad and rude.'

'It is exciting.' I made my hands lay still in my lap. 'I've been doing my best to get my name out there on social media. I felt silly at first, self-conscious. Who am I to scream at people to buy my book? But it's not like that. It's more about interacting, being friendly. I enjoy it now.'

'You *should* shout about it. You went through the effort of researching and writing it. It deserves to be read.'

'Thanks, Mum.'

'Don't forget my two signed copies, one to read and one to frame. My daughter, the author.'

'Maybe you'll still write a book.'

She tutted. 'And go loopy again? Methinks not.'

'You still haven't told me how writing turned you mad.'

'Maybe you can read about it one day.'

I sat up. 'Wait, what?'

'I've started a journal, *not* a book.'

'Okay, a journal.' Excitement moved through me. 'About what?'

'My first mental breakdown. Before I met your father, before I had you.'

'But I thought you said writing...'

'Yes, it turned me loopy. But I think holding it inside is turning me loopier. So yes, maybe one day I will show it to you. Or perhaps I'll burn it. I haven't decided yet.'

I felt like my favourite author had announced a new project. I needed my hands on it *now*. But I knew Mum wouldn't let me see it until she was absolutely ready. 'Please don't burn it. I'd love to read it.'

She looked at me, seemingly about to say something. But then her gaze flitted to the windowsill where the tulips sat: tall, proud, cared for. 'Oh, look at this. We've got a drooper. Give me a sec, Ellie. I can't abide lazy plants.'

I knew it was better to let her get on with it, even though the tulips were fine. She maintained this garden as though keeping it in perfect order would prompt the same flawless functioning in her mind. As if one petal fell, or one plant faded, she would split right down the middle.

5

I have always been scared to look back on the times when my schizophrenia got the better of me. I worry that if I climb inside my thinking process from that time, I will fall completely into it and lose myself. Even now, with antipsychotic medication and after years of therapy, I have to remind myself to stay on the path. The path of sanity, I suppose, because that's what it is.

To the left there is madness. To the right there is madness. I have to keep walking forward.

I still experience the symptoms, but in a muted form. A glance will become a threat, a whisper a secret plan, the sound of traffic the rushing of men coming to get me. The difference is now I have the ability to distance myself from it, to stand at arm's length and say to myself, I am sane, I am not who I once was.

I can't allow myself to fall backward.

But neither can I live with this locked up inside of me anymore.

This is about the first time I went truly mad. It was the mid-eighties, I was a young woman of twenty-three years, and Mother and Father had offered the use of their Scottish cottage for the summer so I could write my novel.

My novel, pah! There was no novel, just the mad delusions of a frantic woman, but I was good at hiding that part of myself from my parents. My father was the owner of a law practice, working fourteen-hour days at times, and my mother was a socialite. Plus I was a woman, not a child, and they were happy to forget I existed unless I reminded them. That suited me.

I'm not sure how to start this. I was in Scotland. There was a typewriter and there was a clock. And there was a soul in the clock. God, that feels strange to write. There was a *soul* in the clock! What sort of nonsensical prattle is that?

The property was run-down, overgrown with nature – so many disobedient plants finding nooks and crannies – and inside it was no better. The walls were cracked and the entire place was ignored. Mother and Father had purchased it years previously amidst dreams of renovating and summering there, but their busy lives had made it impossible.

In any case, my second night I lay on the kitchen floor and I stared at the clock and tried to devise a strategy to remove the soul. (My first night was spent at the upper window, staring out in anticipation of invaders. I believe that is where I first saw the Other.) You see, I had somehow convinced myself the soul was the essence of the house. The reason everything was so ramshackle, I believed, was because the soul was angry.

I know this sounds like babble. With decades separating me from it, I can see that. But at the time this was a very urgent matter. If I didn't somehow free the soul from the clock, the house would crumble around me, crush me, kill me, and then *my* soul would become trapped and I'd be forced to remain there for the rest of my life, my death, if that makes sense.

I had to stop to do a spot of gardening. It is my medicine. Where was I?

The clock – the soul.

I took the clock outside and I crushed it with a rock, smashing the glass face, and then I spread the shards in the surrounding fields. The cottage was a lonely building sitting at the very edge of a village, and I thought by spreading the soul in the verdant fields I would be doing it a favour.

I brought the clock back inside, the glass removed, and hung it on the wall. It continued to tick, but there was no voice buried within the noise, no whispering.

The whispers, the voices... it is difficult to get a non-schizophrenic to understand how *real* they are, how external to myself. They were not whispering from inside my head. They were coming from across the room, from the clock, indecipherable at first.

And then I heard another voice, nestled within the wind. 'Thank you. You saved me.'

But I have never saved anybody. Because I have done evil things, terrible things, things for which there can be no forgiveness.

6

'Good fucking riddance.'

I clasped my hand over my mouth to still my laughter, glancing at the door. It was the Monday after I'd visited Mum and I'd been waiting to give Georgia the news in person. She'd been busy with her family all weekend, getting ready for a camping holiday, so it had to be at work. We were in the break room and, thankfully, it was only us.

'You can't say that.'

Georgia tilted her head at me. She had a take-no-shit face, with wavy blonde hair and a tattoo of a butterfly peeking out from her shirt, an edge of the wing across her collarbone. 'Learning about what that monster did to you, it broke me, Ellie.'

'It was hardly a picnic for me either.'

'But if I'd known sooner...'

'I'm sorry,' I murmured, probably for the thousandth time.

One of the ways Kayden had manipulated me was to cut me off from my friends. Georgia and I had hardly spoken while I was under his rule. But after I finally reached out to her, she helped me to work up the courage to leave him, standing by me every step of the way, helping me get a job.

Kayden had insisted I didn't work, preferring for me to stay at home and clean and sit around and drive myself insane with boredom.

'You don't have to keep saying sorry.' She glared at me, but her twitching smirk diffused it. 'But come on, Ells. You must be happy.'

'He killed himself.' I glanced at the door again, but we were safe. 'He mentioned me in the note, apparently. I should feel guilty, right?'

I was thinking about how Mum had reacted, looking at me like I was poison.

'Fuck. No.' Georgia placed her hands on my shoulders. 'I don't want to hear that again, okay? The only thing you should feel guilty about is that you didn't get to slit that bastard's wrists yourself. God, I wish I'd been the one to do it.'

'Fine, but maybe keep your voice down?'

She laughed in the maniacal way I recognised from secondary school. We'd known each other since we were twelve, Georgia forming part of the gang that had dominated my teenage years.

There was me, Georgia, a few others, and, of course, Theo…

But I didn't let myself think about him, because that led to *the thing*, that ominous annoying taunt in my mind.

'Good riddance,' Georgia said, louder, cupping her hands around her mouth. 'Hope you rot in hell, Kayden, darling.'

We broke into crazed laughter. It felt good to be able to let it out. Georgia was right. Killing him myself was the only thing that would make any of this better. I wasn't going to pretend just to protect Mum's weird fragile sensibilities.

'What's the joke?'

I turned to find Freddy standing there.

He was twenty-five – I knew this because Georgia had not-so-tactfully asked him a few weeks previously – and handsome in a rugged sort of way. His strong jaws were covered with a light dusting of facial hair, and his hair was short on the sides but long on top, casually swept to the side. He clearly worked out, but he wasn't one of those men who seemed desperate to advertise it. He wore his muscles as casually as he wore his creased work shirt.

I felt a flurry inside of me. Suddenly finding anything to say became impossible.

And, of course, Georgia chose this moment to become speechless for the first time in her life. She was gleaming at me, revelling in my discomfort.

'It was a stupid pun,' I said as he strolled over to the kettle. It was the only thing I could think of.

He glanced at me, his lip twitching, his eyes either mocking or alight with something else: something I couldn't entertain, because relationships had never ended well for me. 'I like puns. What was it?'

Fuck. Now I had to think of a pun.

'It was silly. It doesn't matter.'

He clicked the kettle on, turning and leaning against the counter. His shirtsleeves were rolled up and his forearms were annoyingly alluring, drawing my gaze even as I fought it. 'What is it, like, a private pun?'

I tried to tell myself the fact he'd said *like* was a turn-off, that I could never be with a man who was several years younger than me, who said *like*, who I was attracted to for his romance-cover looks. But that was a lie and I knew it. And I thought maybe he knew it too.

'No.' My cheeks were too hot and I could feel Georgia still grinning at me. 'It was...'

Surely I could think of a pun, as a writer, as somebody who

used words on a regular basis. This was getting ridiculous. I blamed it on the kettle's whining, getting louder and louder, and not the thought of how Freddy's prickly-bearded face would feel against my hand.

Suddenly an old joke of Mum's came to me, gifted to me in those rare in-between places when she wasn't turning our lives into a madhouse.

'"I have a split personality," said Tom, being frank.'

He narrowed his eyes at me with a frustratingly indecipherable emotion, and then forced an obviously fake smile to his face. 'Ah, I get it. That's funny, Ellie.'

The moment he turned to the kettle and started making his cup of tea, Georgia began to gesture at him and then me, holding her hands to her chest in a love-heart shape. I waved frantically at her, mouthing *stop it*, but my squirming only made her do it more. She abruptly stopped when Freddy turned, looking between us, perhaps wondering why Georgia looked as though she was about to burst.

'Ladies,' he said, strolling from the break room.

'You are *unbelievable*,' I hissed, shooting her a look.

'God, that was better than TV. I thought you were going to burst into flames! Why did you say a *pun*?'

'I have no idea.' I couldn't help but chuckle, shaking my head. 'It was all I could think of. Your mime show didn't help.'

She pouted. 'Don't get snarky because you've got a crush. For what it's worth, he *so* has a crush on you too. He was staring at you like he'd turn this room into a porno set if I wasn't here. I'm telling you, you and Freddy are totally going to be a thing. He's been eye-fucking you ever since he started.'

'Oh, stop.' I picked up my tea, taking a sip, glancing at the clock and seeing I still had a few minutes before I had to go back. As uncomfortable as this was, it was far better than being shouted at about furniture warranties.

'I'm serious. How long has he been here, four months? Five? He hasn't looked at another woman. He wants you, Ellie. Maybe you should make a move.'

'It would hardly be the most appropriate time.'

She tutted. 'You've been separated from Kayden for over a year. He's dead. He was an abusive monster. You deserve somebody fun, somebody to make you remember life doesn't have to be serious all the time. And I bet young Freddy is *very* fun.'

'I've never been with a younger man.'

Kayden had been older and Theo had been in the same year as me in school. The men in between – the one-night stands and short flings – had been either my age or slightly older.

'You're talking like some old spinster. We're thirty-three, Ells. That's hardly ancient.'

'Maybe I'd prefer to be alone, me and my books. Maybe I'll get a cat.'

'Okay, fine.' Georgia grinned. 'Then invite him round to stroke your pussy.'

'Jesus Christ, Gee, you really are too much sometimes.'

She picked up her tea and blew on it. 'So that's not a no, then?'

I glared at her, but she was right. Despite my protests, it wasn't a no. And that was dangerous. I'd always been a sucker for romance, getting pulled in far too easily, and I knew I had to be extra-cautious after the years spent with Kayden.

But I couldn't deny this feeling in my belly, a silly girlish excitement, when I remembered the way Freddy had looked at me.

7

I was a complaints handler, which translated to members of the public ringing up ostensibly to discuss furniture warranty, but truthfully to scream at me and use me as a verbal punching bag. Georgia advised me to tune it out – they were probably angry at something else, she said – but it was often difficult.

Of course, I longed for the day when I could quit this job and write full time. I wouldn't take Mum up on her offer of supporting me. That was unthinkable and, lately, she'd stopped dropping hints about it, probably sensing how much it bothered me. I refused to be reliant upon anybody else. Digital publishing didn't come with an advance payment, but it *did* come with higher royalties than traditional publishing; my hope was to keep writing and selling until I could make the transition.

I worked at Furniture Care Association because it was a job, and that was that. I'd flitted between positions before Kayden had wrapped me up in his web. For almost four years I'd lived as a prisoner in our marital home, going slowly insane until I'd written a book set within a Victorian insane asylum. Relating to my protagonist had been worryingly easy.

I took a deep breath each time a call came through on my monitor, mentally preparing myself to detach. I couldn't allow myself to become entangled in the nastiness the customers threw my way, hand grenades of vindictive bullshit that could turn me into a wreck if I let them.

I clicked *answer* on my monitor. 'Hello, you're through to Furniture Care Association, Ellie speaking. How can I help you?'

I was using my customer service voice, bubbly.

'Yes, hello,' the man grunted, and then left a long pause.

I waited for him to go on, but he only breathed down the phone, heavy and jagged. The sick thought came to me he was touching himself, but I ignored it. Perhaps he had respiratory issues. I always tried my best not to judge people, knowing there was plenty to judge about me.

'Hello, sir? How can I help you today?'

No notes had come through with the call, so I had to assume this was a new complaint and he'd been blindly passed to me from another team. The other departments had an annoying habit of referring to us for the smallest issue.

'Sir?'

'What's your name again, girly?'

I bit down for a moment. Girly. This guy was a creep. 'My name is Ellie, sir. I work in the complaints department. Do you have something you're not happy with?'

'Ellie, nice name. Yeah, I've got a complaint.' His breathing got quicker, more ragged. 'I need you to sit down on my face, girl, sit down nice and hard, and then pump those slut hips until you're squirting into my mouth–'

I clicked *end call* and pulled off my headset, closing my eyes and doing a little self-talk for a minute or so. I told myself I didn't need to get angry, didn't need to get upset, didn't need to be human in any way.

It was over. It was nothing.

I opened my eyes to find Georgia looking at me over the desk partition. She was on a call, but she offered me a thumbs up. I smiled and nodded, giving her the okay sign, even if my heart was doing a jig in my chest.

Kayden had hurled words like that at me, endless torrents of his sickest delights. *Moan. I have to fucking believe it. Let me know how close you are, baby. Make sure to cream on that dick. I want it* soaked, *angel. Can you do that for me?*

I breathed. I focused. There was nothing I could do but carry on with my job.

The day went on as usual: monotonous, boring, an exercise in clock-watching with me and Georgia pulling faces at each other every chance we got.

She kept throwing a look to the other end of the office, toward the mailroom where Freddy worked. I glared at her, even if part of me enjoyed it, even if my overactive mind was imagining what it would be like to claw onto Freddy's forearms and see if they were as rock solid as they looked.

The man called again at half past three, using a different name so I didn't get any advance warning it would be him.

'You want it.' His breathing was unmistakable. I swallowed a sickly feeling. 'You were made for it.'

'Sir,' I said firmly, 'if your query isn't related to a warranty claim or a complaint, I'm afraid I'm going to have to hang up on you.'

'That's an idea. *Hanging.* I'll choke your cunt neck as I take you raw–'

I ended the call again.

Frantic energy buzzed around my body, urging me to scream or throw something or bolt from my chair. I'd never understand what twisted pleasure some men derived from this sort of behaviour, why it made them feel big to make women feel small.

But I wasn't the scared shivering state in Kayden's bed anymore. I wouldn't let myself crumble.

No sooner had I ended the call than another one came through, this time from a customer I recognised.

I spent the next half an hour arguing with Mr Patel about his three-piece suite, an issue we'd gone over dozens of times before. We were waiting for some parts to be shipped from China and he refused to understand how it could take six weeks, so he rang up every Monday to check if they'd arrived. When he learned they hadn't he blamed me personally and we went around and around in circles.

Normally I dreaded talking to him, but today it was welcome after the freak.

But then, an hour later, another call came through from a customer I didn't recognise.

I swallowed, my throat dry, my belly tight with nerves.

'Hello, you're through to Furniture Care Association, Ellie–'

'Listen here, you horny fucking slut–'

'No, *you* listen.' I slammed my hand against the desk, causing my keyboard to leap up, pens to jostle about. 'If you say one more revolting thing to me, I am going to find where you live and call the police. Do you understand? You'll be arrested for sexual harassment, you sad fucking–'

'Ellie!'

I cringed at the sound of Nigel's voice, thrown at me from across the other side of the room.

I turned to find him standing at the door to his office, his hand gripping the frame. Nigel took his job as seriously as a military commander, a man of around fifty with neat hair and a tucked-in shirt. He stared hard at me, and I resisted the urge to yell at him. He was so up his own arse, brimming with his own importance. It was pathetic. He was going to make me feel like dirt for standing up for myself.

'My office.'

I sighed in resignation, dropping my headset on the desk. 'Of course.'

Standing, I exchanged a quick look with Gee. She was staring at me in support, but there was nothing she could do. She was already on Nigel's hit-list for a prank she'd played a couple of weeks ago. That was the sort of man Nigel was: treating a whoopee cushion with the severity of a landmine.

Why did that dickhead have to choose me to call, of all the employees in this place?

Perhaps it was related to my increased presence online, I reflected as I made my way across the office, dozens of eyes tracking my dreaded walk. Nigel was notorious for his rants. The power-tripping prick.

Perhaps the caller had stumbled across one of my many Facebook or Twitter posts and googled my name.

The thought sent a nasty twisting feeling through me.

That meant *anybody* could be watching me.

8

Nigel paced up and down his small unimpressive office with his hands behind his back, behaving as though he was an army general and I was his troop. 'You have to understand how your performance reflects on the business as a whole.'

'Yes, I get that.' I sat while he stood, which I was sure he enjoyed. 'I don't know what came over me. But that customer–'

He spun on me. 'The customer is *always* right. Have you ever heard that phrase?'

'Yes, I've heard it.'

'And do you believe it?'

'Frankly, no, no I don't. But I shouldn't have sworn at him. In my defence, he was masturbating and saying very lewd things to me.'

'Enough excuses!' he roared, redness creeping up his neck and across his cheek.

I sat back and settled in. I'd learned over time how best to deal with Nigel: let him tire himself out.

He'd rant at me for five or so minutes now, roaring at the top of his lungs to make sure everybody could hear, and perhaps that made him feel good when he went home to his family. Perhaps he bragged to them. *Had to put a couple of my troops in line today*, and he'd ignore the disinterested way they glanced at him, the resigned way, because each of them wished he was somebody else, somebody less pathetic, less obsessed with himself.

I knew I was being bitter, but I didn't feel guilty about it. I despised being forced to sit there and take his crap.

'Well?' He smiled cruelly, reminding me of Kayden, the way his eyes would glimmer before we began whatever game he'd invented that night. 'Don't you have anything to say?'

'I shouldn't make excuses, I guess.'

'You *guess*?' More redness: more bluster. 'You guess? What the fuck is that supposed to mean? You've put the whole company in jeopardy. What do you think happens if word gets out our complaints handlers – who are supposed to be the *friendly* face of the company – talk to our customers in such a despicable way?'

I sighed.

'Oh...' He folded his arms, tapping his foot. 'Am I boring you?'

Knock-knock.

He wheeled around at the interruption, his hands trembling as he paced across the room and pulled the door open. 'What?'

'I reckon that's enough now, mate.' It was Freddy, his Midlands accent pitched low. 'She's got the point. You don't need to make a song and bloody dance of it.'

Warmth rose inside of me, followed by an acid tinge. He'd ridden to my rescue and part of me wanted to thank him, but there was another part – a resentful part – that screamed he didn't have the right. We were nobody to each other, and I had to keep it that way, or else...

Or else Theo. Or else Kayden. Or else everything would turn to shit, like it always did with men.

Not that my feelings about it mattered. Freddy was about to get the mother of all tongue-lashings now he'd entered the arena.

'Um,' Nigel said.

I sat up. *Um?* Nigel never sounded unsure. He was an idiot and took himself far, far, *far* too seriously, but I'd never heard him say um.

'What does that mean?' Freddy snapped.

Nigel sighed heavily, turning to me with the bravado draining from his face. 'Go on, Ellie. Get back to work. And try not to swear at any more customers, all right?'

For a moment I sat there, too stunned to react. I had no idea what had happened, why Nigel was listening to Freddy: the lowest of the low, the mailroom boy, who'd only worked there a few months and wasn't past probation yet. My thoughts spiralled to visions of violence and blackmail and pain, perhaps because that was how Kayden had always kept me in line.

Perhaps Freddy tightened coarse rope around Nigel's wrists, pulled and pulled until he could feel each thread of the rope cutting into his skin, a thousand sizzling lashes. And then he strung him up, and he took off his belt – slowly, always slowly, so he could hear the *click-click* of his wedding ring against the buckle, and then, and then...

But no. I needed to shut my fucking head up when it came to that stuff.

It was obviously more mundane. Nigel always took out his rage more on the women, and I'd never seen anybody confront him before. Maybe he needed to be put in his place.

'Okay,' I said sceptically, rising to my feet. 'Thank you.'

I strode to the door quickly, as if Nigel would slam it in my face if I didn't move fast enough. He *did* slam it: behind me, and then he stomped loudly across his office.

Freddy grinned at me, his hands in his pockets. 'Isn't it *me* you should be thanking, eh?'

I was close enough to smell his aftershave, or it could've just been his scent. It bothered me, just as the way he was staring at me was vexing. I could feel people peeking over their desks at us, snatching glances, as though this was a romcom and they were viewing a budding romance.

But I wasn't going down that road again.

I stepped forward, lowering my voice to a hiss. 'Save your gestures. I don't expect them and I don't need them.'

I hurried across the office and dropped into my chair, exchanging a look with Georgia. *What the hell?* her expression said. *Why aren't you being chewed out right now?*

I shrugged. I had no idea.

I already regretted snapping at Freddy. I was replaying the conversation in my mind, wishing I'd reacted differently, hoping I hadn't upset or offended him.

I knew that was a problem, something I needed to solve.

I couldn't – I didn't – care about Freddy Jenkins or his muscular forearms or his aftershave or his perceptive captivating eyes or *anything* about him. Even if he'd ridden to my rescue like a knight in shining armour. Or a knight in a devilishly crumpled suit.

I. Did. Not. Want. Him.

That was my story and I was sticking to it.

9

One of the first traditions I reclaimed after leaving Kayden was reading at the seafront. I refused to allow the fact I'd met him there cloud the enjoyment it brought me. There was something therapeutic about sitting on the stone benches, families all around me, dog walkers strolling by as the setting sun kissed the horizon.

The first time I'd returned, I felt sure he was going to spring up from some unseen place, that just-Kayden smirk on his lips, a smirk that said he owned me and he always would. I was his property. He could do whatever he wanted with me.

I brought out my Kindle. I was plotting a historical fiction novel set within a medieval convent and I was reading quite a dense book for research. It required lots of concentration. I stared and willed the words into some kind of order, but my attention wavered, my thoughts moving over what a strange day it had been.

I still didn't know what to make of the pervert who'd rung up and asked for me specifically. But more confusing was the way Nigel had crumbled the moment Freddy confronted him, within seconds. *Poof*, and I was free.

Or if my thoughts didn't stray to work, they flittered over to Kayden and his gaping wrists, the carmine tatters they must've been when Paisley found him.

Did it make me happy she was the one who'd discovered his corpse? And if it did, was that really so wrong?

My Kindle screen had locked while I stared at the ocean blankly, like the catatonic mental patients who'd populated my first novel. I was about to swipe it open when I noticed somebody swaggering over to me, something bunched in their hand, and for a mad moment I was sure it was a bomb of some kind. It was the intent with which they walked: ready to throw, ready to do harm.

The man was either homeless or cared very little about hygiene. I tried to withdraw judgement as he got closer, but there was no denying how rough he looked. It was difficult to tell his age with the dirt crusting his skin, the lankness of his hair, the emptiness of his eyes.

He stopped just shy of me, and I saw the apparent weapon was really a crumpled-up newspaper. 'Spare any change, Ellie?'

'I'm sorry, but I don't carry...'

I didn't carry cash, because I had no need of it these days. I used contactless payments for most things.

But he'd said my name. Like he knew me.

I tried my best I-mean-no-harm smile and nodded to the newspaper. The local had been kind enough to offer me a space to publicise the release of my book. 'I take it you saw the article?'

'Yeah, I saw it. I read the whole fucking thing. Because even a piece of filth like me *can* read, darling.'

His tone was bitter. He took another step forward and I found myself sitting upright, staring him in the eyes, the same way I'd learned to do with Kayden. I couldn't seem scared, because he'd liked that.

'I'm sure you can. But I don't have any money.'

'A big old publishing deal and you can't give an honest man a couple of quid. You uppity fucking cunts are all the same.'

Anger pulsed inside of me, but it was buried deep, beneath layers of fear and restraint and certainty I'd lose if I chose to play his game. 'I don't think I deserve to be spoken to like this. I'm leaving.'

I gathered up my bag and walked toward the closest group of people I could see, a family of four crowded beneath a pop-up tent. It was a warm evening, the sun taking its sweet time setting, and thankfully the beach was busy.

'Stuck-up whore,' the man yelled after me.

I walked as quickly as I could without drawing attention. Bizarrely, shamefully, I felt embarrassed even if I'd done nothing wrong.

I imagined sprinting back there and spitting in his dirty disgusting face for making me feel small. Or chopping his cock off and shoving it down his throat.

But instead, I walked, my work shoes clicking loudly on the promenade, trying to convince myself everything was fine and there was no danger of my drumbeat heart getting out of control.

That fucking prick. That animal.

What right did he have to talk to me like that, to make me feel like nobody?

There were so many little Kaydens in the world, treating people horribly and getting away with it. It drove me insane.

I didn't consider finding another spot on the beach and returning to the book. There was no point. It clearly wasn't my day. I headed toward the bus stop, ready to lose myself in my writing, the one thing which always made everything else drift away.

10

There was something magical about sitting down at my desk with my fingers poised over the keys.

It would've been smarter of me to live in a one-bedroom property, considering that my wages weren't fantastic. But I loved having a place that existed solely for my craft. I loved the print I'd hung above my desk: a watercolour of a forest at night, the trees silhouetted by steely moonlight.

I loved how empty it was: my desk, the chair, and my computer. There were a few more prints on the walls – nature scenes, nothing distracting – but there was no more furniture. The only messiness was my paperbacks, piled up in the corner.

It was a land of zen, of concentration, separate from the discarded clothes and dirty dishes and general lifeness of the rest of my flat.

I played some soft jazz and opened up my files. I liked to have my chapter outline on one side of the screen and my manuscript on the other, so I could refer to it whenever I needed to.

And then...

Heaven, oblivion, nothing but me and my characters. Their

worries became my worries, their reality mine, and there was no person called Eleanor Salter.

There was no Kayden and there was no whisper turning to aggravated groaning when I told him no. There was no, *Come on, honey, put some effort into it.* There was no tightening of my spine when he brought a forkful of food to his mouth, no tragic relief when he told me I'd done a good job tonight. There were no shattered plates and there was no rape and there was no violence and there was no shame that I should've acted sooner, should've saved myself the moment he revealed his true nature.

There was this word-made world and nothing else; the rest of life ceased to matter. That was what writing was, why I loved it, why I could be locked in a windowless cell and still find solace if I had a strong cup of coffee and a word processor.

Time bled as I wrote, as it always did, two hours passing in what felt like two minutes. I only stopped when my rumbling belly told me I should probably eat something. That was another good thing about becoming obsessed with stories. For me, it was one hell of a diet tool.

I saved what I'd done, backed it up, and closed my eyes. My brain felt tired, well-used, which was good. Hopefully I wouldn't have to replay the events of the day endlessly when I tried to sleep.

I pushed away from the desk and stood.

I turned.

Kayden stood at the window, grinning from ear to ear, staring right at me.

11

His bright blue eyes stared at me, *into* me, the same way they had when he loomed at the beach and changed my life with that ensnaring smile. I stumbled backward, letting out a jagged breath.

And then he was gone.

As suddenly as he'd appeared, he'd vanished, as though turning to smoke. I blinked and realised there were useless pathetic tears in my eyes: the sort of tears which had never helped me before, which had probably made it all the more fun for him.

'*Go on, Ellie, cry on that dick.*'

Memories stabbed me as I paced through the flat, charging to the front door like my life depended on it. And perhaps it did. Or, at the very least, my sanity was at risk.

I *had* seen him, hadn't I?

Or maybe I was tired, overworked, overstressed.

Maybe the coward victim part of my mind agreed with Paisley, blaming me for Kayden's suicide, and it was throwing up phantoms to torture me.

I pulled on my shoes roughly, cramming my feet into them.

'*You always were an obedient slut. You can't tell me you're not enjoying this.*'

I paused at the door, massaging my temples, trying to steady my breathing. I hated myself; it was time for action, to do something, and there I was playing the narcissist just like Mum. An onrushing panic attack was more important than chasing Kayden, apparently. I breathed slowly, calming down, wishing I could just be normal.

What did it matter?

If he'd been there, he was long gone.

Or he was waiting out there for me, a knife tucked up his sleeve, ready to do to me what he'd pretended to do to himself.

I breathed slowly, measuredly, counting in for ten and out for ten.

Once I'd managed to bring myself under some sort of control – hating myself every second for being a psycho who needed to remember to *breathe* – I unlocked the door and pushed it open.

I did a quick circuit of my ground-floor flat, around the small communal garden area that nobody bothered with much. I thought about looking at the grass to see if he'd left any footprints, but the window to my office was on the roadside, on concrete.

I peered down, trying to detect any scuff marks, a cigarette butt, anything to prove Kayden had been there. There was nothing but a bare patch of stone and a creeping feeling up my spine, a whispering at the edge of my consciousness that I had gone mad before and I could do it again.

'Stop,' I whispered, clenching my fists as I walked back toward my flat. 'Stop.'

Saying it aloud was a way to push back the rising memory, to stomp on it until it was bloody and stopped fighting. I never allowed myself to so much as glance at that corner of my mind, lest the monster within get encouraged by my gaze, stirring and cannibalising every part of me until there was nothing left.

I hurried inside and locked the door, using *all* the locks. I normally took some solace in the satisfying metallic noises they made, but this evening all I could think about was the way Kayden had stared, face distorted by glass and light, so that he was part Kayden and part my reflection. Part Kayden and part me.

As I wandered through my flat turning on every light, I thought about that.

Part Kayden and part me.

It was entirely possible I'd seen my own reflection in the glass and then, fuelled by fear and anger and maybe a touch of unfair guilt, I had superimposed that evil bastard's face.

If Kayden had faked his own death, I couldn't imagine him having the self-restraint to simply appear at my window with a smile. He was the sort of man who needed immediate violent gratification, the sort of man who needed to wrap his hands around a woman's neck to maintain his erection. His sadism was deep-rooted, a broken part of a broken person.

Or perhaps this was the beginning.

Paisley would lie for him, wouldn't she? She'd *say* he'd killed himself, he'd mentioned me in the note, even if he hadn't. I hadn't seen the body or the death certificate and Paisley had made a point of saying I wasn't welcome at the funeral.

I dropped onto my bed and laid my head in my hands.

I was starting to sound like Mother. It was the way she'd ranted in the weeks following Dad's death, covering our living-room walls with printouts from various news websites where people had miraculously recovered from cancer. 'You see.' She'd waved her hands manically. 'He wants to make us happy, and when are you happier than when you realise what you lost, it isn't lost, it's right there. You get it, Ellie? You get it.'

It wasn't a question at the end. It was a statement said with a tinge of anger, the rage incomprehensible to my young mind, but I'd grown to understand it as I grew older.

The fear of madness had always gnawed at the edges of who I was, had always made me question myself, which was why I couldn't let myself devolve into conspiracy theories where Kayden was concerned. It might turn me the same way as Mum: a wall covered in haphazard research and a head filled with absurd untruths.

What was more likely, Kayden had faked his death only to sneak down here and grin at me for a moment or two? Or I'd seen my own reflection in the glass and had freaked myself out, the same way I had dozens of times before?

There was a hole in my childhood, a Theo-sized hole, an entire year of my life missing.

One day I was fourteen and then I was fifteen, and I was left with no idea what the past year had held for me, except that Theo and his family had moved away and Mum had somehow returned to something like her old self.

When I awoke from that fugue, that year of amnesia, the world's longest blackout... whatever the fuck I called it, when I awoke, I knew Mum was expecting me to argue with her. It was in her eyes, the anticipation of a struggle. She at least thought I'd ask some questions.

Why am I in a mental hospital? What happened to me? Where is Theo? What is going on?

But I never asked, because the pain in my mind, the screaming voice that told me to look away from that year, to whatever happened to me, it was too sharp. That was the *thing* I sometimes thought about: the shotgun blast to my memory, eradicating whole pieces of me.

Georgia must've known, but she never said anything. I was home-schooled for my final year and then it was off to the world of part-time jobs in Bristol, to one-night stands, to drugs and partying and pretending I was happy when I was anything but.

I could've found out. I could've made Mum tell me. I could've done some research with my old classmates.

But I never had and I never would.

Whatever it was, it was too terrible, too painful even at the edges. It was worth sacrificing an entire year of my life to never have to look at it. My mind had deemed it necessary to lock it away deep inside, a Pandora's box that could never be opened, otherwise it might wreck me.

And that was how I knew, with absolute certainty, that it was far more likely I'd imagined Kayden in the glass.

12

There are some things about schizophrenia we will never talk about, because... Well, because it's not something other people will understand. One of these things is how madness can sometimes be fun. There were times in the midst of my psychosis when I could harness whatever was happening to me, and I could *use* it! (At least, I thought I was using it. It was probably using me all along.)

I am not talking about madness like sweet Eleanor went through. I was thinking of that earlier, when I was searching the attic for some of my dear late husband's photographs. I felt sure there were some up there, but I stopped when I came across *it*, or maybe it should be a capital – I, *It*, like the Stephen King book, but there was nothing clownish about this photo.

It was of Ellie in the midst of her psychotic break, her hair in disarray, staring at the camera as though she's afraid her eyeballs are going to fall out of her face. I still feel guilty for taking that photo, which is why I never sent it to that poor boy Theo. I should have burnt it. I *should* burn it, but there's something sick about burning a photograph of one's own daughter. I've put her through enough without setting her on fire.

Does she hate me for never telling her what happened, why she broke with reality?

Here's what the doctor said, more or less.

'Psychotic breaks, madam (he was a proper sort of gentleman, with a stiff back and a pointy nose and big glasses)... they are, or they can be, a defence mechanism of sorts. The mind is skilled at protecting its vehicle from harm, even harm from itself, if you see my meaning. (Of course I saw his meaning.) If it believes a person has become so hopeless they may harm themselves, it will detach from the hopeless event. I am not implying this is a conscious decision from some internal *other*. (Other, Other. What a word to use. You may meet the Other.) It is an automatic process in extreme and rare circumstances, as reflexive as snatching your hand away from a hot stove you thought was cold.'

That's what my sweet Ellie did. She detached. She removed herself from what happened and what led up to it, and she never asked about it. She avoided school and she avoided her friends and she avoided life if it connected to what had happened. I'm impressed she's gone this long without stumbling upon it, but our town isn't a small village. It's big enough to hide. And part of me suspects if somebody *did* tell her, she would simply refuse to hear it. To protect herself.

When I was in Scotland, in that godawful run-down cottage, I would escape and take walks in the surrounding countryside. It was a beautiful place, with thick woods and long open fields and always a breeze stirring. I would often walk the same route at the same time each morning: a regularity that was my downfall. But perhaps it would have ended the same anyway.

I walked through the woods and listened to the wind in the trees: the talking wind, the way it would form words and whisper and say things. And sometimes these were threats, insults, whole speeches about how impure and unworthy I was. In those instances I would turn and run away, locking myself inside the house which, if it was scary, at least was a familiar fear by then.

But other times the voices would be my friends, laughing along with me as I hung from tree branches, goading me as I sprinted through the woods. I would sit cross-legged on a tree trunk and close my eyes like some meditating monk, and I would let them filter into me and give me ideas for my book.

I felt sure I'd tapped into some magic way to write a book, a new method that would launch me into superstardom. I know how ridiculous that sounds. Magic indeed. But that is the mind of a schizophrenic, or at least it was *my* mind when my illness was at its most potent. I believed I was the centre of all things, that everything was spinning around me. I was above God and nature and everything, everybody.

I was too good for the regular rules, for the law, for common decency.

Oh yes, I was the special young woman in the woods, the fairy-woman, skipping around with her magic voices and her unrealistic dreams and her supreme self-belief, and it was wrong, what I did, how it ended, where it led me. It was wrong.

It was wicked and evil and I wish I could take it back.

But sitting there in the woods with the voices of my friends around me, I felt strangely at peace. I felt – I dare say – more *me* than I'd ever felt before or I've felt since. How odd that I was able to block out the rest of it, tear whole pages from my mind, right until the very end.

Which makes me something of a monster considering what came after, *who* came after, and the pain I inflicted.

When I set out to write this journal, I promised myself I would be completely honest, and that's a promise I intend to keep. But honesty comes in shades. I am going to be honest to *my* experience: to the order in which things happened to *me*, not the order in which they truly occurred. In the mind of the psychotic these are often very different things.

For the first time in my life, I am going to tell the truth about what happened between me and my daughter's husband.

13

The next day at work, there were a couple more calls from the pervert saying disgusting things to me down the phone. He seemed to delight in calling me every name that could be hurled at a woman, getting cruder and meaner the more I maintained my professional façade. Georgia was on annual leave with her family, holidaying in Cornwall for a few days, so I didn't have my best friend for backup.

'Think you're special because you've got a shit book coming out, do ya? Think anyone's really gonna read that bollocks?'

I hung up after giving him ample warning, which was a requirement in this job. We didn't have the right to satisfyingly slam the receiver down. All I could do was click *end call* with as much passion as I could muster.

I took my fifteen-minute break alone, sitting in the corner of the break room with my Kindle and a mug of much-needed coffee.

It was strange, perhaps, how easily I'd come to accept seeing Kayden in the glass. But my mind *was* strange, a landscape I never liked to delve too deeply into unless I was writing, and I wasn't going to spend too long questioning my own sanity. I might not like the answer.

I looked up from my Kindle when Freddy swaggered in, moving with that casual confidence that infuriated me. He *slinked* over to the kettle, moving like a jungle cat or something, as though he had all the time in the world.

With his back to me, I was free to study the way his shirt pulled tautly from shoulder to shoulder, the way his muscles twitched at his smallest movements. He was waiting to explode into action any second, and my mind flooded with all the actions he might perform. I imagined him spinning on me with that annoying smirk, his eyes glimmering.

You want this, he growled in my mind, *stop fighting it*.

'Getting a good look there?' He spooned coffee into his mug. 'I'm happy to pose if you've got anything special in mind.'

'What?' I stared at my Kindle. 'I have no idea what you're talking about.'

He turned to me, folding his arms. Why couldn't he roll his sleeves down? I'd never been so fascinated by forearms before. 'Come on, Ellie. I could feel you undressing me with your eyes. It's all right. You don't have to be ashamed.'

'Do you always have to be such a prick?'

He chuckled, holding his hands up. 'I'm the one who saved the damsel in distress yesterday. And what do I get for it, eh? Shouted at in front of the whole office. How's that for grateful?'

My cheeks burned. I affected my best glaring don't-give-a-fuck face. 'I'm not a damsel. And I don't need saving.'

He shrugged and returned to his coffee, making the process last far longer than he needed to. I couldn't stop myself from studying him, the way the sunlight slanted through the window, resting on his face: the edge of his mouth, always twitched upward as if he knew the punchline to a joke I couldn't guess at.

I thought he'd leave once he'd finally finished, but instead he swaggered over to me and dropped into the seat opposite. We exchanged a look – his smirk widened – and then he took a long, slow sip of his coffee, keeping his eyes on me the whole time.

It was so weird, I couldn't help but laugh. He grinned and laid his mug down. 'Mission accomplished.'

'What, your mission was to stare at me like a freak?'

'To make you laugh. And I succeeded.'

I rolled my eyes and tapped the Kindle's screen, turning the page. 'Good for you.'

'What are you reading?'

I scoffed, hating the noise the moment I made it. I sounded pretentious. But it *did* seem an absurd question coming from him. 'Why?'

'Goddamn, Ellie. *Why?* It's a simple question.'

'I'm reading a book about how madwomen were treated in the Victorian era.'

'Oh yeah? And how were they treated?'

'Terribly.'

He nodded. 'Makes sense.'

'How does that *make sense*?'

His grin widened, wolfish. His musky cologne was far too strong, washing around me. 'Those men had important stuff to do. The last thing they needed was a bunch of hysterical women running around ruining everything for them.'

'You're an asshole, Freddy. Has anybody ever told you that?'

'Only about a hundred or so.' He shrugged. I wished I could care as little as he did. 'So, when are you going to let me take you for a drink?'

I laughed, hating the sound. It was the same way I'd laughed when Kayden had stared down at me that day on the beach, when he started his Nice Kayden routine, turning on the charm to crumble my defences. It was my *flirty* laugh. There was something here, something primal and urgent, and I was trying to fight it. But it was difficult.

'I might be a tad old for you. But thanks for the offer.'

'Come *on*, Ellie. I'm twenty-five. You're thirty-three. How is that so bad?'

'I guess you've been talking to Georgia.'

'She said you were worried about the age gap and I had to subtly make you understand I didn't give a damn. Here it is: my subtle hint. I don't give a fucking fuck about our age gap, all right? You're beautiful. You're funny. You're interesting. Let me take you for one drink, Ellie.'

I made a mental note to send Gee a vicious text and royally ruin her good mood in Cornwall. But I couldn't deny the truth. His words were sending feelings flurrying around my body, waking up parts of me I'd promised to put to sleep after Kayden. The *thing* with Theo – waking up after a year with no idea where he was or what had happened – was bad enough. But Kayden had been worse.

I couldn't risk myself with another man, not so soon.

'One drink.' He laid his elbows on the table, staring hard. 'I'm not going to pounce on you. I'm not going to pressure you. It's just... come on, you must know I like you. I haven't exactly been subtle.'

I turned my gaze down, resenting the flush moving across my cheeks. 'I guess you're not very subtle in general, are you?'

'Nope.' He chuckled. 'And I'm not ashamed to admit it. Life's too short.'

'Says the boy.'

'The age thing again? Goddamn, if it makes you feel any better I'll invent a time machine so we're the same age.'

I giggled. I *giggled*. I had to stop. 'And how would you go about doing that, hmm?'

'For you I'd find a way.'

I mimed gagging. 'Do those lines work on your other girlfriends?'

'My *other* girlfriends?'

'Girlfriends,' I corrected. 'Forget I said *other*.'

'But, my sweet damsel, I don't think I can. It seems to me you're keener on this than you're letting on.'

I groaned, but it wasn't a leave-me-the-hell-alone noise. It was the groan of a woman who was interested, and I couldn't stop myself from smiling at him.

It was one date: one drink. Surely I was allowed a little fun after all I'd been through. I wouldn't let my guard drop. I'd die before I let another Kayden into my life.

'I don't understand why...'

'Why what?' He leaned closer, our hands almost touching on the table. His eyes pinned me in place. I loved the way he was looking at me, with total attention. 'Why I'd want to take you out?'

I bit my lip. I nodded.

I wasn't the most drop-dead gorgeous woman in the world. I wasn't the smartest. I wasn't the most successful. I was definitely not twenty-five years old anymore. I knew thoughts like these were cruel and counterproductive, but that didn't mean they didn't flurry around my mind, self-hating arrows flung here and there.

He reached across, our fingers brushing. I felt it then. Sparks. I felt the sparks. People talk about that all the time. But I truly felt it when his fingers moved over mine.

'Because you're you, Ellie.'

I snatched my hand away and forced a laugh, but it came out garbled and wrong-sounding. 'Do you have any idea how cheesy you are?'

He sat back, his eyes more serious than usual, his smirk replaced by a soft frown. 'I mean it. I've wanted to ask you out ever since I started. But believe it or not, you're pretty intimidating.'

'I struggle to believe you could be intimidated.'

'Fair point. I am pretty badass.'

'I did *not* say that.'

'One drink. Don't make me get on my knees and beg.'

I wondered what it would be like with his thick arms around me, or showing up at a party in a glittering dress with Freddy made more handsome in a suit. I imagined his lips on my neck, kissing down toward my collarbone, and a shiver moved through me.

'*One* drink,' I said. 'And I mean one.'

'Of course, Ells. I'll respect your boundaries.'

'Ells?' I cocked my eyebrow at him. 'That's the first time you've called me that.'

He stared. Freddy was good at staring. 'Are you complaining?'

I picked up my Kindle. 'Please leave me alone so I can read in peace.'

'Friday. I'll leave my number on your desk. Text me yours and we'll arrange it. And *Ells*... if you stand me up I *will* cry.'

'Ha, ha, ha,' I muttered as he left the office.

I waited until he was gone and set the Kindle down, grasping my hands together, trying to fight the budding excitement rising inside of me. But it was impossible.

I hadn't been on a date since Kayden and I had separated. I hadn't masturbated, worried if I allowed myself to indulge, Kayden would emerge cruelly into my fantasies. It was a sick thought. But he was the only man I'd been with in years, the only skin I'd felt, the only person whose body had fused with mine. It had been an ugly fusing, a caricature of affection, but it was still the only intimacy I'd felt in years.

I should've known better.

But the truth was I was looking forward to the date already, abandoning my book so I could think about what I was going to wear.

I promised myself: one drink. That was all.

I couldn't let myself be duped by Freddy's charm the same way I'd been snared by Kayden.

14

My life quietened down over the next few days. Except for the occasional perv caller at work, I was able to return to my regular routine of writing and getting ready for my book launch. I was beginning to feel excited as the big day got closer, the butterflies in my belly reminding me of how I'd felt leading up to my wedding.

But when Friday evening came, as I settled down at my window – forty-five minutes before my date with Freddy – I felt sick at the thought of how excited I'd been. I remembered how I'd let my mind flood with thoughts of mine and Kayden's future, stupidly convinced he'd remain Prince Charming after he got the ring on my finger.

Freddy was charming, the same way Kayden had been, and for the millionth time that week I promised myself I would take things slow with him.

I looked over the sea at the setting sun, taking a deep breath and letting the glittering view calm my nerves.

After a sip of wine – there was no way I could face my first date in years stone-cold sober – I took out my phone and went to Goodreads.

My publisher had given out advance copies to dozens of readers, meaning they got to read the book early in exchange for an honest review. I knew many of these reviewers through Facebook, and some of them had already reached out privately to tell me they'd enjoyed it.

I almost spat wine when I saw the rating.

Two stars.

Two fucking stars.

There were more reviews on there than I'd expected: almost a hundred. It didn't make any sense. We hadn't given out that many copies.

I scrolled to the bottom of the page and scanned them, my belly cramping. There were seven reviews from names I recognised, five five-stars and two four-stars, but the rest were from people I'd never heard of, who couldn't possibly have read my book.

This is the worst book I've ever had the misfortune of reading. I can't believe the author thinks this is acceptable.

If I could give this zero stars I would.

Immature writing, pathetic plotting, poor editing.

Drivel, complete and utter drivel.

I hope this author never gets the chance to release another book.

Hahahahaha, is this some sort of joke? This book is terrible.

I dropped my phone on the table, the sound seeming far louder than it had any right to be.

I stood and paced, wringing my hands together, knowing

this was a dangerous sign. As a woman who'd lived on the edge of madness her whole life – with a missing year and schizophrenia waiting to burst into my personality – I'd learned the warning signs of mania.

Pacing was one. Squeezing my hands together so hard they hurt was another.

Was Paisley behind this? Somebody had clearly arranged to have my book review-bombed, which meant people who'd never read it were giving it one-star ratings. It had happened to a few authors who'd been in scandals, but I hadn't done anything wrong. I hadn't made a fool of myself publicly.

I could imagine Paisley rubbing her nicotine-stained hands together as she read these. I could imagine Paisley and Kayden sharing a bottle of wine as they read them out loud to each other, laughing in that strange way they had, that too-close way.

They'd always had a bizarre relationship. One Christmas, Paisley had kissed her son on the cheek when he'd brought in the Yorkshire puddings, but the kiss had lingered far too long, and then afterward she'd licked her lips and given me this skin-crawling look, as if to say, *He was mine first, bitch. He'll always be mine.*

After Kayden's father died of cancer – a similarity we'd bonded over before he'd revealed his true self – it was like she'd transferred her affections to her son. It was sick, but Kayden had always assured me I'd imagined that look.

That was Kayden: gaslighter extraordinaire.

The thought struck again. Kayden had faked his death. Kayden was toying with me.

But it didn't make any sense.

Kayden had stayed in Scotland for a year, leaving me alone, never showing his face. And he wouldn't need to fake his own death to do any of this: to hire people to yell at me down the phone, homeless people to accost me in public, reviewers to pillory me.

I forcibly stopped my pacing, cautioning myself to slow my thoughts down.

Perhaps Paisley was behind this as revenge for her son's death. She'd said Kayden had mentioned me in his suicide note. That would make some sort of sense, I supposed, even if it was psychotic reasoning. But if Kayden was alive, I couldn't imagine him playing it this subtle.

I thought of the glass: of his face in the glass.

'I'm not like Mum,' I whispered. 'I'm not fucking *mad*.'

I picked up my phone, meaning to call my publisher, but I couldn't resist another look at the reviews. It was foolish and I knew it, but I read them all, every scathing one.

I've read more sophisticated prose in a children's book.

This wannabe Fitzgerald isn't fooling anyone.

Terrible from start to finish. There isn't a single redeeming quality.

I swiped off the page, not daring to look on Amazon.

My mind filled with violent vivid vignettes: stabbing Paisley in her neck, turn her folds of flesh into crimson tatters; kick and punch and hurt something, anything until I didn't have to think about those reviews anymore.

The other stuff – the creepy callers and the homeless guy – I could put that down to my very minor celebrity around Weston since my book had been announced.

But this was a targeted attack.

I navigated to Blakelyn Younger's name on my phone. She was the head of my publishing house. One of the benefits of being with a smaller publisher was I had her phone number.

She was an approachable person, but even so I felt guilty for ringing on a Friday night.

But the ever-reliable Blakelyn picked up.

'Ellie?' There was murmuring in the background. A cork popped and somebody clapped. 'Hello? Can you hear me?'

'Yes. I'm sorry to ring so late.'

'No worries. What's up?'

'Have you seen my Goodreads page?'

There was a pause as she walked outside, a door opening and closing, causing the background noise to become more distant. 'No. I don't tend to. We have so many authors. Why, is something wrong?'

I quickly told her about the one-star reviewers. 'They haven't read it, have they? Did we give out more advance copies or something?'

'No, no. We only give out fifty. It's impossible these people have read it. I don't understand why anybody would do this.'

'Neither do I.' I laughed humourlessly. 'I haven't done anything. Online, I mean. A scandal. Not that I can think of.'

A man's voice rose in the background. 'Come on, Blakey, the cake's ready. We need you to blow out the candles.'

'Oh, God. Is it your birthday?'

She laughed drily, with perhaps a touch of annoyance nestled within the sound. Or maybe I was imagining that part. It wouldn't be the first time my mind had played tricks on me. 'Yes, but please don't feel guilty. When I told you I'm on call twenty-four-seven, I meant it.'

'No, I'm sorry.' I hadn't released a book yet and there I was bothering the boss on her birthday. 'I shouldn't have called on a Friday night.'

'I'll look into this first thing on Monday. I have no idea what's going on. Give me some time to get caught up and we'll knock it on its head, whatever it is.'

No way. I couldn't leave those reviews up for an entire weekend.

But making a fuss had never been something I was good at. It was like the times I'd imagined telling somebody – a teacher, a friend – about what was happening at home when I was growing up. I simply couldn't summon the words.

'Of course.'

'Ellie, I mean it. We'll sort this.'

'Come on,' somebody yelled in the background, a woman's voice this time.

'It's okay.' I paced over to the window, laying my forehead against the glass. 'I'm sorry.'

'You don't need to apologise. We're here for you. I mean that, Ellie. We've got your back.'

'Thank you. That really means a lot. And… Happy birthday.'

'Speak soon. I'll let you know the second I've got a handle on this.'

She hung up and, stupidly, I turned right back to the reviews. Even if I knew Blakelyn was right, even if I knew there was no chance these people had actually read my book, each word stung. Each word convinced me they were right. I was a terrible writer. I'd poured innumerable pieces of myself into my work, and I'd failed.

It was foolish. The more experienced writers at my publishing house told us newbies not to take things personally, but it wasn't as easy when it was my book baby they were criticising.

My phone vibrated.

I swiped quickly, almost dropping it in my urgency.

It could be Blakelyn with news.

But of course it wasn't. She'd probably put her phone on *do not disturb* so I'd leave her alone.

It was Freddy.

Hey, hot stuff. Still on for 8?

I debated telling him no. I wasn't up to it.

But what else was I going to do, sit around the house reading about how terrible I was?

Yes. I'm leaving soon.

15

The reviews were still bouncing around my head as I climbed from the taxi and headed down the street. The seafront was busy this time of the evening, legions of partygoers heading toward the myriad bars that lined the promenade. When the weather was like this – pretty much perfect – and the bars were packed, it was easy to imagine I was abroad.

It reminded me of the time Kayden and I had gone to Turkey, in the early days before he revealed the teeth behind his smile.

We'd jaunted through the shallows together, hand in hand, with my stupid naïve giggles filling the air and his deep laughter making me feel loved, hopeful for the future.

I hated it, where it would lead: spiderweb patterns of pain across my thighs and my belly and my back, always places people wouldn't notice.

But he was dead. *Dead*.

And perhaps his sick mother was taking it out on me.

I wondered how Paisley had arranged the reviews. Had she paid for them?

'Ellie.' Freddy walked out behind me, grinning. He'd had a shave and a fresh haircut, shorter on the sides now, the top swept over in a way that made me imagine running my hand through it. 'Lost?'

I returned his smile as best as I could. 'Sorry, I was miles away.'

'No need to apologise when you turn up looking like that. Hot *damn*.'

I laughed at his forwardness, waving a hand, even as his compliment ignited something in me. I'd spent a fair amount of time choosing my skinny black jeans and sparkly gold top, and it was nice to have the effort noticed. 'Thank you. But please, what did we say about cheesiness?'

'I think your definition might be different from mine.' He casually placed his hand on the small of my back, his touch burning against my skin, as though there was no fabric to protect me. I should've told him to remove it, but I didn't. 'Shall we?'

He led me to a table in the corner of the outside seating area. Fires flickered within metal grills and blood-red rugs were laid here and there, making me think of the laundry I'd done countless times in my marriage – my imprisonment – to Kayden.

Blood-red sheets, blood-red shirts, blood-red, blood-red, blood-fucking-red and he never once said *sorry*.

Freddy tilted his head. 'Are you all right?'

'Just thirsty.' I forced another smile. The reviews had stirred up too much, hit me in my most sensitive area. I remembered what Blakelyn had said: *we'll sort this*.

'What's your poison?'

'A glass of rosé, but please let me get it.'

'What?' He chuckled, narrowing his eyes. 'I might be a kid in your eyes, Ells, but I'm old-fashioned when it comes to ladies and their drinks. I insist.'

'Really...'

He sprung to his feet. 'Back in a sec.'

I watched him go, studying the way he held himself. He was wearing a denim shirt and chinos, and he wore it well. I noticed several ladies sneaking glances at him as he passed by.

My fingers itched for my phone, but I knew I'd only return to Goodreads to torture myself some more.

I looked across the promenade instead. There was a railing on the beach wall, built in the last decade or so. It hadn't been there when I was a child.

A hand gripped the railing and I stared at it, stared at the gnarled hand and the gold watch, and I knew it was Kayden, Kayden's hand and Kayden's watch, because I was very familiar with those hands and he'd always made a point of taking off his watch before beating me.

'Do you think I enjoy this?' he'd say. 'I wish you wouldn't make me. Really. I don't want to do this. Can't you understand that?'

The worst part was how convincing he'd sounded, as though he meant it, as though he truly prayed there was a way for him to stop. But there had been. He could've just... *stopped*. But instead, he'd leapt upon me with feral intensity every time.

The owner of the hand pulled himself up the final step.

And of course, it wasn't Kayden.

It was an older man with grey hair and a salmon-coloured checked shirt and his wife followed him a moment later.

I told myself I wasn't going mad. I wasn't Mum. I was stressed and tired and understandably anxious. That was all.

I'd imagined the hand belonging to Kayden the same way I dreamed up his face in the window a few nights previously.

Freddy returned with my glass of wine and his beer. He took a slow sip and sat back, looking at me with that I-have-a-secret way of his.

I took a large gulp of wine, eager for it to numb me. 'I hope you weren't waiting too long. My taxi was late.'

It was the only thing I could think to say.

'Ells, I'd wait ten years for you.'

I laughed despite myself. It was the way he said it, with heavy irony, as though he was auditioning for a play. 'Do you always have to be weird? Let's have a regular conversation.'

'What exactly is a regular conversation?'

'I guess you could tell me about where you grew up.'

'Wolverhampton. When I was four I had a pet hamster called Chucky. There was a postbox right at the end of my street and…' He trailed off, chuckling. 'That enough detail for you?'

'Come on. It's a fair question.'

'Who cares where I grew up? I sure as hell don't. My childhood isn't relevant to me.'

'I'm sorry. But that is literally an insane thing to say.'

'Why? Don't tell me you're one of *those* people, walking around with a chip on your shoulder because some bad stuff happened when you were a kid.'

'No,' I said, taking his comment seriously even if he'd said it with his usual veil of sarcasm. 'I hate that. I try not to do it. I fail sometimes. But I try.'

'Me too.' He raised his bottle. 'Here's to failing. Here's to trying.'

I raised my glass and we clinked them together. 'So do you have anything to say about yourself? Or are you going to make vaguely philosophical comments all night?'

'We're not all as interesting as you. I had a look at your website the other day. Your book sounds fascinating.'

I placed my glass down before I squeezed it to shattering. Normally I'd love to talk about this, but with this review craziness, it felt too fragile.

'I refuse to believe you want to work in furniture claims your whole life,' I countered, changing the subject.

'That's where you're wrong. As a kid, I used to dream about

entitled pricks shouting at me because their futon has a coffee stain on it. Really. I used to purposefully spill drinks on people's sofas so I could get some experience.'

It felt good to laugh, and it was easy with Freddy. I shook my head at him and I felt myself wearing a flirty face: pouting lips, fluttering eyelashes, a come-get-me expression I hadn't worn in years. I certainly had never encouraged Kayden's advances, not after I learned what he was truly made of. I'd made myself as ugly as possible, often not showering, taking little care in my appearance. Sometimes it stopped him; most times it hadn't. 'You're either hiding a massive secret or you're the most boring person in the world.'

'Maybe I'd prefer to talk about you.'

'Everything interesting about me is on my website.'

'So a person can be summed up in a two hundred word bio, can they?'

'Yep.' I grinned widely. 'So why don't you tell me, in two hundred words or less, exactly who you are.'

He shrugged. 'I was raised in a pretty okay family. I played rugby as a kid, and for a while I thought that was going to be my path in life. But then I tore my meniscus, badly. Like, really fucking badly. Do you know what that is?' I shook my head. 'It's this cartilage in your knee. I was bedbound for a long time. Maybe I could've recovered from it, had another go at it. But I was a kid and it seemed like the end of the world. That's when I discovered the guitar.'

'You play?'

'I don't make love to it, if that's what you're asking.'

'Dick.'

He chuckled. 'Yeah, I play, if you can call it that. I was in a band for a while but it fell apart. It was a real Beatles situation, classic really. A girl got between us and...' He stopped, a dark look coming over his face when his phone started to ring. He took it out of his pocket and scowled, swiping forcefully to quieten it.

'Bailiffs?' I tried to make it sound jokey, but part of me wondered if it had been another woman ringing him. I had no right to be jealous, but I silently wished his phone wouldn't ring again.

'No, it's... nothing. I signed up for this betting website and they've given my number to half the companies in England.'

I took another sip of wine, realising my glass was almost empty. Had he lied to me? I couldn't think why he would, unless it *had* been another woman. But again, that wasn't my concern. This was a casual drink, nothing more. I certainly didn't own him.

'So you fell out over a girl?' I prompted, remembering his comment before the phone had interrupted us.

'Yeah, exactly.'

'Who won?'

'In the long run, he did. In the short term, I split from the band and moved to Weston with the girl. Then we split. She moved back up north to be with my mate.'

'Oh, I'm sorry.'

'Why?' He looked out to the sea. 'I love this place. And if I didn't stay here...'

'Nope.'

He arched his eyebrow. 'Nope?'

'Yeah, *nope*. I refuse to allow you to make another cheesy comment.'

'Who said I was going to?'

'You were going to say, *If I didn't stay here, I never would've met you.*'

'Jeez, talk about having a big head.' He reached across the table and prodded me playfully. But playful or not, his touch lingered, tempting. 'I was *actually* going to say if I didn't stay here I never would've learned what it's like to live in a place with such a lovely crackhead community. Honestly, they're a great bunch.'

We laughed. He had a point. Weston was beautiful, but there were fifteen or so rehab centres and we attracted addicts from all over the country. Some of them rehabilitated, but many dropped out of their programmes and roamed the streets instead.

Our gazes met. There was a definite moment, a definite understanding between us. We both knew – without saying it – where this night could lead if one of us urged the other. More drinks: maybe a club. And then we'd fall into each other's arms and the rest would take care of itself.

But I didn't want that. Rather, I didn't *want* to want it.

'Freddy, I think I really might make this just one drink. I... I do like you, but, well, the truth is this is my first date in a long time. A *long* time. And I'd prefer if we didn't rush things.'

'Hey.' He held his hands up. 'I meant what I said, Ells. I'm never going to pressure you. I hate weasel blokes who pull that shit. But here's the deal. I'll only let you go if you agree to two next time. And that's *minimum*.'

He thrust his hand across the table. I took it, shaking it for far longer than was necessary. His eyes seared into me as we held on to each other.

We both felt it. We both hungered for it.

'Deal.' I tried to laugh away the intimacy, but it came out wrong-sounding. 'And I can always drink the rest of this one *suuuuper* slowly.'

He lifted his beer. 'I think I'll join you with that.'

We beamed at each other as we competed to see who could make their sip the most ridiculously long, Freddy coming out the clear winner when he placed his bottle down in slow-motion, complete with sound effects.

16

I did far more walking than writing that summer. I'm not sure I ever had it in me to be a writer. I remember when I was mad – the second time I was *really* mad, I mean – I would ask sweet Eleanor to sit at my typewriter and write: just type, I'd told her, and she'd done as I asked because she was a kind and loving girl even after everything I'd put her through.

What she doesn't know is how my mind would make the moment shimmer, an image distorted through glass, and suddenly I'd be staring at *myself*, not my daughter. I could imagine my fingers were skittering across the keys. Sometimes I felt the sensation against my fingertips, pawing at the air as she typed.

These are the sorts of unearthly things I felt in those days, and yet, deranged or sane they are some of my most cherished memories. Dear Ellie would always beam proudly when she finished a page, holding it up in the air.

'Mummy, Mummy,' she would cry. 'Look what I did.'

I'd hold her. I'd love her. I wasn't all bad, was I?

Listen to me, delaying the inevitable.

I did more walking. I did little writing.

And on one of my walks through the nearby woods I met Kayden. A chance meeting in the woods, with no hand to steer us, either of us. Pah!

I thought he was one of my characters at first. I would oftentimes run into these apparitions when I was out on my jaunts. They would skip by, offering me a giggle and a wave.

Children would clamber up trees with ungodly speed and suited suitors would smile invitingly at me from deep within the underbrush. Eyes would gleam from tree bark, and I'd understand without asking – the only way I knew anything in those days – they were there to offer me inspiration for my novel, the work that would reshape the world.

I was a silly young woman, I confess.

Kayden was a handsome young man, with deep black hair and sharp eyes. Sometimes, in my sillier moments, I mourn how grey that gorgeous hair became. What a fool I am, what a horrid broken fool. He had a haunted look about him, and there were clouds, literal black clouds, shifting and teasing around his head. They called out to something deep within me.

And the whispers, there were whispers, but I cannot absolve myself. I refuse that escape.

He was shirtless. It pains me to admit I liked his shirtlessness. His body was taut and strong and his belly was flat and back then my predilections were something grotesque. What is stronger, I ask, the internal or the external, nature or nurture? Me or the *Other*?

He'd tied a sturdy piece of rope around a thick tree branch and fashioned the other end into a noose, and he was walking up and down in front of it, flexing his fingers and glancing at it every few moments. There was a definite air of him building up to something. He'd placed a tall log beneath the noose, presumably so he could kick it away once he'd slipped his head inside.

And what did I do?

What did I do when I saw this muscled young man ramping up to his suicide?

I am sick. I am twisted. I am wrong. I am broken.

I do not want to write what I did, because it would be far better, wouldn't it, far more civilised if I'd called out to him and asked if he was okay. I should have told him, no, no, you silly young man, step away from there at once!

But if I am to do this properly, I must include everything, the depraved details that would never make sense to a sane mind. There are things I could include, explanations I could offer, but they would not be true to who I was *in that moment*. In that moment it was just me and the boy, and I was excited, grinning and salivating.

So here is what I did: I watched him pacing, and I watched the interplay of light against his muscled body, and I slid my hand into my knickers and I touched myself until I dragged a sad orgasm out of me. And then I kept touching myself, lost in the strange allure of it, obsessed with the way he was pacing, and then it was like the pacing was directly connected to the functioning of my hand, through some ethereal force, and as with everything else I did not question this.

I had multiple orgasms watching a young man preparing for his death.

And of course, this is the part where you ask yourself why, how. It isn't a normal thing to find pleasure in such pain. It isn't a normal thing to indulge the dark aspects of oneself so readily, but I made a promise to tell this story as I experienced it. I cannot tell you why I felt so much jagged ecstasy at the sight of his near death, not yet, not until the right time.

Or is that an excuse, a way to justify this reprehensible thing?

Oh, how I rubbed, how I stroked, how my wet cunt pulsed and the shivers moved through me. I do not like to curse, not usually, but that's what I was: a sad, pathetic ugly monster with a sickeningly wet cunt and a sickeningly shattered mind.

Do not think I am setting myself up for redemption. For, despite the circumstances that might later be revealed, there is no excuse for what I did. There is no excuse for any of it.

People make small talk with me in garden centres and I have civilised lunches with ladies I met at bingo and I visit the library twice a week to restock my reading material. All of this is to say I am a regular older lady, I believe, if such a thing exists. On the outside: my shell is the same as any other.

I am rambling.

God, I hate it, I hate that I did that.

My whimpers of release eventually alerted him to my presence.

His expression turned immediately from savage and ready for death to a convincing smile, so convincing I felt sure I'd mistaken the noose's purpose. He looked far too happy.

'Are you okay over there, lady?' he said, and his accent was delightful. It was thick despite his youth, confident despite his desire for self-destruction.

I emerged from the forest, moving like I was the queen of the world. I had supreme self-assurance in those days, unearned and undeserved, but it was there all the same. I held my head high and tipped my nose up as though my knickers weren't soaked and sticky. I was a pretender, even to myself.

'Says the man with the noose,' I said to him.

And he said to me, 'This isn't a noose. It's for pull-ups. Look.'

He leapt up and gripped onto the rope and started doing one-armed pull-ups, grinning at me all the while, in that way of his, that uniquely Kayden way, as though the rest of the world was not a passing thought in his mind. He casually switched hands and did some more, and I could see he knew the effect he was having on me.

I ducked my head and sprinted straight at him. It was the sort of deranged thing that seemed entirely logical to me at the time.

He laughed and dropped down, but not quickly enough. I was a fast girl in those days. Before he could say a word I had him pinned against the tree. My hands were clasping his face and I brought my lips close to his, but I did not kiss him. I held them there and I stared into his eyes and I smiled very widely, very strangely.

I asked him to tell me why he planned to kill himself. I said if he didn't tell me I would dig my fingernails into his neck until he had no neck left.

He laughed, and there was hunger in his eyes, sweet and vile hunger.

He told me his father was away for work much of the time and his mother was... and then he paused. He looked past me into the forest as though she might be standing there, as though she might be watching. 'She tries her best,' he said to me after a long time. 'But her best isn't exactly something I enjoy. Get my point?'

A little bitterness there: an arrow flung. But it would never hit its mark. It was an impossibility.

I let go of his face and stepped back. 'I think I get your point.'

In fact, right then it flooded into me: what his mother did to him, how she crept into his room and rode him as he wept. At the time I knew this was divination, transcendental knowledge touching me. At the time I thought I could read minds.

'What's your name, lady?'

I told him I was called Lottie. He smiled in that perfect

terrifying way of his, a smile that would compel anybody inclined toward the male sex: that would drive anybody feral, as it drove me into animal thoughts, into carnal obsession. I had a very high sex drive in those days, and his smile was encouraging me greatly.

But I was also the daughter of two very proper parents. I'd been raised to never make the first move with men. I believe this is the only reason I didn't kiss him right there.

'I'm Kayden,' he told me, 'and I think you've given me a reason to live.'

17

'So, how was it?' Georgia asked, smiling at me over the top of her coffee mug.

I glared at her. It was the Monday after my date with Freddy and she was back from her holiday in Cornwall. I hadn't rung to confront her about scheming with Freddy, mostly because I was secretly glad she'd done it... not that I'd ever let *her* know that.

I blew on my tea. 'It was nice.'

'Just nice? Come on. Give me the juicy stuff.'

'There is no juicy stuff. We had one drink. We shared a couple of laughs. And I went home.'

'But you like him.' Georgia looked closely at me, her eyes bright. 'You *really* like him. I can tell.'

'Maybe I do. Maybe I don't. I need to take it slow.'

She nodded. 'Of course, Ells. At your own pace. You don't have to rush into anything. Although if I was you I'd ride him until his balls looked like shrivelled prunes.'

'Gee!' I laughed as a blush touched my cheeks. 'You're insufferable.'

She grinned. 'Yes, yes I am. But seriously, I'm glad. You deserve to have a bit of fun.'

She was talking about Kayden, of course, and the hell I'd hidden from her. I wondered if I was doing the same by not telling her about the reviews and my dead husband's face in the glass, but I failed to see what telling her would achieve. There wasn't any news about the Goodreads situation, and the face in the glass had been tiredness and stress, nothing else.

For some reason, the mad urge rose in me to ask her about the *thing*, the gap in my memory.

I forced it down. I'd never look there. I'd never look *close* to there.

'Am I interrupting?' Nigel strode into the break room, hands behind his back. 'Ellie, a word. My office.'

He spun and marched away, and Georgia aimed her middle finger at his back. 'What's that about?' she asked once he was gone.

'No idea.' I stood. 'But I'm guessing it isn't good.'

'It never is with that prick.'

I walked from the break room to Nigel's office, glancing briefly toward the mailroom where I knew Freddy would be. I hadn't seen him since our drinks on Friday, and a needy part of me whispered it was unfair. He should've reached out. I had to remind myself we'd agreed it was a casual thing, no big deal. He didn't owe me anything.

I knocked on Nigel's door and he met me with a terse, 'In.' He nodded at the door as I pushed it open. 'Close that behind you.'

I did as he asked and walked across the office, sitting in the chair opposite him. Of course, he stood the moment I sat, looming over me with his stiff upper lip and his erect posture and his supercilious air. 'Can you tell me why we've received half a dozen one-star reviews on Trustpilot and other websites about our service, and why *your* name has specifically been mentioned?'

Fucking *Paisley*.

She'd gone after my dream job – writing – and now she was going after the job I hated. I would've thanked her if I didn't need to pay my rent.

'What do the reviews say?'

He paced, brushing down his shirt, as though there were crinkles in the material when truthfully it looked as though he'd ironed it a hundred times. 'You're unprofessional. Your telephone manner is rude. You called one customer a word I refuse to repeat. These are serious allegations. They reflect poorly on the business. We need this to stop.'

I massaged my temples, forcing my breathing to come slowly. I pictured Paisley's wide smile and that foul twinkle in her eye: a twinkle that said she would do anything for her precious baby boy, her sweet do-no-wrong Kayden.

'Well?' Nigel snapped.

'I think these reviews are from one person, using different accounts. Or she's paid people to leave them. The same thing has happened with my book on Goodreads, a bunch of one-stars appearing out of nowhere.'

'I didn't call you in here to discuss your side hustle.' He leered. 'And please, no excuses. Your performance has been subpar for a long time. I can't remember the last time you hit a bonus performance target.'

'With all due respect, Nigel, I was under the impression the performance targets were optional. That our main focus was on keeping the lines flowing and keeping the customers happy.'

He flinched. 'Yes, technically they are–'

'And I also disagree that my performance has been subpar for a long time. Nobody has mentioned this in my quarterly reviews. I haven't been told I need to improve my performance by anybody.'

'Fine, fine.' He waved a hand. 'If not subpar, then far below what I think you're capable of.'

I shrugged, staring silently at him. We both knew he had no actual ground to stand on here, except for his opinion. But we both also knew that confrontation was not something I relished. He must've sensed it during my time here: the way I'd never asked for a raise, the way I'd keep my head down and try to glide through this dreary nine-to-five as uneventfully as possible.

'But why wouldn't you try to reach for the stars,' he went on, 'instead of sitting in the gutter?'

I almost rolled my eyes. He spoke in such a ludicrous way. *Reach for the stars.* Withholding payouts from confused elderly women who thought buying warranty really meant their furniture would be repaired – only to find out they'd been conned from the start – was hardly my idea of reaching for the stars.

'We can't have our business slandered on these websites based on the performance of one employee. You need to buck your ideas up.'

'Nigel, honestly, the same thing has happened with my book. I think somebody is–'

'This has nothing to do with your *book*.' He swiped his hand through the air. 'Nobody wants to hear about your goddamn book. It distracts the other employees. It makes them think...'

He left it hanging, but I knew what he meant. It made them wonder if they could pursue their own hobbies instead of letting this place grind them down.

Laying my hands on the table, I looked at him as steadily as I could. 'These reviews are not genuine. The same thing has happened elsewhere. They don't accurately reflect the opinions of our customers.'

'It doesn't matter.' He gritted his teeth, released them. It seemed to pain him simply looking at me. *Why?* 'They're on the website. Other customers can see them. Whether or not they're real is beside the point.'

I wasn't going to get anywhere with him. I'd have to go to the source. I'd have to ring Paisley, which would be torture considering I'd hung up on her the last time we spoke. She'd love making me squirm over that.

But I had no choice.

My book, my work... and I'd bet on her being behind the weirdos ringing me up, and maybe she'd paid that homeless man to accost me. Or was that paranoia coming out to play? This sort of thinking was too conspiratorial for my liking.

Fine: maybe not the homeless man. Maybe not the pervert callers who'd, thankfully, decided to leave me alone for the time being.

But she *had* to be behind the reviews.

Nigel laid his fists on his neat desk. 'And don't think your *friend* can save you, either.'

'Who, Georgia?'

'Pfft. No. Freddy. That arrogant... don't think because he can get away with his bollocks, the same applies to you.'

'Why is Freddy allowed to get away with his bollocks?'

Nigel dropped his gaze, making me feel like I'd gained ground, maybe an inch or two. 'He isn't. He doesn't.'

But that was a lie.

Ever since Freddy had begun working at the company, he'd shown up late on several occasions, sometimes missed entire days, often made mistakes that would've provoked a signature Nigel tirade from anybody else. I understood it less after the showdown the previous week, when Freddy had stared Nigel down and ended my tongue-lashing early.

It made no sense, and a part of me wondered if Freddy *had* something on Nigel, some dirt that meant he was allowed to get away with more than most. Or perhaps Nigel and Freddy knew each other from outside work. I had no clue. Nigel was normally strict: less so with the men than the women, but stern all round.

'But you said–'

'Enough, Ellie. I didn't bring you in here to talk about Freddy.'

'But you brought it up–'

'*Enough.*'

We met eyes for a moment, something unreadable glinting across Nigel's expression. Perhaps I could've pressed the matter: dug and dug until I was at the heart of the issue. Perhaps I could've tried harder to work out what was really going on. But, unfortunately, that was not in my nature, though I often wished it was.

'Sort those reviews,' he said finally. 'If you're telling me the truth, prove it. Get them removed.'

'I will.'

I left his office quickly, my heartbeat hammering far too insistently.

This was a targeted attack, and there were only two people I could think of who'd harass me like this: Kayden and Paisley. Kayden was dead, I knew, I *knew*, because if he was alive he'd make me physically squirm, hurt me in ways that left marks on my flesh. He wasn't the sort for petty games. It must've been Paisley.

As I walked across the office, another thought cut me sharply.

What if *Theo* was behind this?

I had no idea what had happened between me and my childhood sweetheart to cause him to leave. I hadn't let myself speculate about it, because that would mean exploring avenues of my mind best left ignored. I might wander unknowingly into the truth. I couldn't risk that.

But if I'd done something to Theo – something so evil

nobody in my life could bring themselves to confront me about it – perhaps he was out for revenge.

I'd searched for Theo on Facebook a few times over the years. He was living in London and working as a graphic designer. His profile photo showed him smiling cheekily at the camera, the London Eye glinting in the background.

What was I thinking?

Of course it wasn't Theo. He probably never thought about me.

I had to ring Paisley. I had to stop this madness.

18

After work, I sat in the living room with my phone balanced on my knee. I could track the nerves moving through me by the way the phone trembled, in time with my twitching leg, somehow remaining balanced despite the shaking. Perhaps that was my life, I reflected: quivering, on the edge, but remaining poised in the most unlikely circumstances...

My phone fell, clattering against the floor.

'Shit.'

I was glad I'd invested in a screen protector, wiping it with my sleeve once I'd picked it up.

I knew I had to ring Paisley and get to the bottom of this, but the idea of speaking to her made me feel sick, physically sick, bile churning in my stomach. We'd only met a few times during the years I'd been married to her son, but each time she was more vicious than the last, looking at me like I was her competitor rather than her son's wife.

Kayden had told me I was conjuring it up, that there was something wrong with me for letting my mind go there. But she looked at her son like a *toy*. I knew I hadn't dreamt it up.

I navigated to her phone number, going to my call history to find it. I didn't have her number saved. If I had my way, I'd eradicate her and her son from my life forever.

I put the phone on loudspeaker and stood up, pacing up and down the living room, my chest getting tighter with each successive ring.

'Aye?' she snapped, answering.

'Paisley, it's me. It's Ellie.'

'Well, well, well.' She drew it out, savouring it. 'Rung to apologise, have you? Hanging up on your mother-in-law after her son's – your *husband's* – death. That's the lowest of the low.'

I stifled a deranged laugh. Apologise? The woman was out of her fucking tree.

'I need to discuss something, something very troubling that's been happening to me lately. I think you might know something about it.'

'Nah-uh.' She tittered, then let out a jagged smoker's cough. 'You have to say you're oh-so-sorry for hanging up on me.'

'I don't think–'

'You're the reason my son is dead!' she screamed, sudden violence making the phone crackle. 'The least – the *very* least – you can do is say you're sorry. Or are you really that low? Are you really that pathetic?'

Her son had once tied me to the bed for an entire day. I was forced to piss and shit on myself, to lie there in my own filth, and when he returned he'd wiped me down and... and then he'd taken what he thought was his, what he thought he deserved. I'd been so crippled with terror I'd *moaned* for him: moaned as he instructed me to, desperate for him to finish.

I was *pathetic* for not mourning that fucking lunatic?

I clenched my fist and stared at the phone. 'We don't have to fling insults at each other. Let's try and speak like grown-ups, please.'

'*Ooooh*, aren't you Miss High and Mighty?'

'It was you, wasn't it? The reviews?' Anger shivered in my voice. I couldn't help it. I felt an eruption coming, the way my emotions always emerged: violently, suddenly, or not at all. 'You paid some fucking losers to review my book, because your sad, freak, sadistic fucking *nothing* of a son did the world a favour and slit his wrists. Didn't you? *Didn't you?*'

There was a long pause and then she let out another titter. 'I really have no idea what you're talking about.'

'Don't lie to me.'

'Oh, fine. Maybe there's a *wee* part of me that wants to make you pay for what you did to my son. Maybe watching you swan around on Facebook with your pathetic fans bothers me. But what are you suggesting, that I had one of my internet-savvy friends find me a service where you can pay to have books, what's it called, review-bombed? Is *that* what you're suggesting?'

There was glee in her voice, a caricature of a proud little girl, her gravelly smoker's tenor incongruous. 'And are you *really* suggesting I also paid to have you poorly reviewed on professional websites for your workplace? Really, Ellie, you're as mad as your mother.'

'You fucking bitch.' I almost threw my phone, stopping myself at the last moment. I raised it and screamed into it. 'You dirty, disgusting fucking *paedophile*.'

She flared. 'You're a sick girl. To call me *that*... All I ever did was love my son. All I ever did was care for him. And now he's gone. Because of you. Do you really think I'd let you get away with that?'

'So you're admitting it was you?'

'Oh, I wouldn't go that far.'

'Paisley, you need to stop. You can't do this to me.'

'Stop what? I haven't done anything.'

'You admitted it!'

'I have no idea what you're talking about.'

I groaned and dropped onto the sofa, my leg twitching manically. 'Please. I want to put the past behind me.'

'That's not your choice to make, girl. The past is the past. It always catches up.'

So she was a philosopher now. She was driving me insane.

'Do you know what I think?' I snapped. 'I think Kayden's still alive. I think he's pulling the strings. Because you, you sick perverted cunt, aren't clever enough to think of any of this.'

'How dare you!' she cried. 'I was the one who found the poor boy. You have no idea what I saw. He was drenched, you silly girl, *drenched*. There was blood all over the floor. There was blood smeared across his face. The note had blood on it. You weren't at the funeral. You didn't see them put him in the ground.'

'Yeah, whatever you say.' I was being vindictive. And yet part of me honestly doubted what she said. Part of me truly believed Kayden's face in the glass hadn't been my imagination, even if I knew this was dangerous thinking, Mum-like thinking. 'I bet he's there right now, rubbing your feet in that special way you like. You ruined him, Paisley. You say you love him, but you broke him, and he went on to break others.'

'All I ever did was love my son–'

'He told me what you did,' I lied. 'All those times you'd sneak into his bedroom...'

'He didn't tell you a fucking *thing*,' she raged, but I could hear the uncertainty in her voice. I knew I was right. I'd always been right. This woman's whole existence was a mistake. 'All I ever did–'

'Yeah, yeah, save it for someone who cares. Stop this stuff with the reviews or I'm going to contact the police.'

'If I did what you're claiming, do you really think I'd leave evidence of it anywhere?'

'Say hi to Kayden for me.'

'You're a monster, Ellie. To taunt a woman with her son's death, a suicide *you* caused, is plain evil.'

'Your son was – *is* – a monster.'

'Come and visit his grave if you think I'm lying. Maybe you can't accept what you did. My sweet Kayden only ever wanted to do good. You deserted him. That's the worst thing a wife can do.'

'I escaped an abusive bully. Stop the review-bombing or there will be consequences. I'm hanging up.'

'There's nothing you can do, girl. Nothing you can do to stop what's coming.'

'What's that, Paisley? If your rapist son is really dead–'

'Don't you *dare* call him that–'

'What the fuck could you possibly do to me?'

'You'll see. Oh, how you'll wish you said sorry.'

I hung up and tossed my phone onto the sofa cushions, leaning back and letting out a groan. I stared at the ceiling, at a spot of damp in the corner, a few flecks that would soon spread and corrode the whole flat if I didn't do something about it.

The phone call hadn't gone as I'd planned, except I was now fairly certain Paisley was behind this.

But she'd given no indication she would stop. And my threat of ringing the police was a bluff, because I knew they could do nothing. They would take my statement and promise to look into it... and, if Paisley had done a passable job at covering her tracks, they'd find nothing. That was if they looked into it, which they probably wouldn't.

Was paying for a book to be poorly reviewed a crime?

I wasn't sure. I didn't think so.

I closed my eyes and saw Kayden staring at me, his gaze searing through the darkness of my eyelids, his smile vicious and victorious.

Even in death, the bastard was winning.

19

I tried to focus on my writing for the rest of the evening, but sitting at my computer was difficult. It was too easy to open the internet browser and torture myself by combing over the reviews. Fake or not, each word stabbed me. Their very existence was a bad sign for my novel's success.

It wasn't as though a potential reader would know they were fake. This whole thing was not something I'd ever dreamed of having attached to my first book's release. Dragging more words out of myself felt impossible.

I couldn't get to that place, the flow state, the not-thinking-just-writing mood where the words would begin to pour out of me. I was the sort of writer for whom contemplation was death. I couldn't ponder or overly think about what I was doing, or I'd end up dissecting every word until there were no words to dissect.

It might've had something to do with how I'd first started, hammering at Mum's typewriter as she goaded me on. 'Just write, just write, just keep writing...'

I pushed away from the desk, spinning idly in the chair. I'd pulled the curtains shut ever since Kayden's face had appeared, intent on not letting it happen again.

Visit his grave if you think I'm lying, Paisley had said.

Was she telling the truth? If I drove up to Scotland, would there be a grave marked Kayden Hunter?

Hunter: perhaps the most fitting name ever given.

I sighed. I stood.

My mind was spinning far too quickly. It wouldn't settle.

My publisher hadn't contacted me, so either they were busy or they were still looking into it.

My phone buzzed from the desk. Freddy had sent me a text.

Thinking of you.

I smiled as warmth shimmered through me. I tried to fight it – I was done with romance and men and the heartache it brought – but I couldn't deny how special that was. After the day I'd had, Freddy found a way to make me smile. That mattered. It was significant.

I texted him back.

What did I say about being cheesy?

He wrote back almost immediately.

Nothing cheesy about the truth. Wanna hear something else that's true?

Go on…

I may or may not have something to confess.

What do you mean?

I pressed *send* and wandered into the living room, closing the office door behind me. I knew I wouldn't get any writing done that evening. It didn't help that my subject matter was madness and delusion, a theme that felt far too close.

I poured myself a glass of wine and took a small sip, dropping into the armchair as Freddy replied.

I'm not sure I can tell you, Ells. You might be offended.

Now I HAVE to know.

I stared as the three dots teased me, vanished, and then reappeared.

Let's say it involved thinking of you in some less-than-professional situations…

Tingles moved over my body, up my thighs, swirling in my belly. I hadn't felt this in years. I hadn't *let* myself feel anything like this, because it would risk leading to other things. But when the choice was between obsessing about Paisley's sick games and sinking into the searing lust Freddy prompted in me…

I found myself itching to be close to him, wishing he was there with me. It was bad and I wished I could fight the feeling.

Instead, I took another sip of wine: made the sip longer, tipped the glass up until I'd emptied it entirely. I wasn't much of a drinker and immediately my head got cloudy, my body more receptive, the idea of sinking into this feeling less intimidating.

I wrote back, fumbling a couple of times before clicking *send*.

What situations?

Do you want specifics?

I slid my hand slowly up my leg, wondering if this was it: the first time I'd touch myself in years, the first time I'd allow myself this release.

Yes, Freddy. I want specifics.

Three dots appeared... vanished, appeared again. I imagined him lying on his bed, shirtless, his young fit body throbbing with as much need for me as I felt for him. I imagined him laying his torso against me, feeling the hardness of his chest, feeling his hot breath on my neck.

All right, Ells. But only because you asked nicely.

We both lost control, texting each other frantically, the scenario getting dirtier and steamier and so hot in the end I could hardly stand it.

I rubbed myself furiously as my blurry gaze moved over his words, each one coming in quicker than the last, like they were thrusts instead of texts.

He was there: fucking me with his promises, letting me forget about Kayden and Paisley and Theo and my shattered memory and my sabotaged career.

All I had to think about was Freddy, about the things he was going to do to me, and the pulsing wetness between my thighs.

In the end I was a gasping wreck, collapsing back onto the chair with my legs twitching, vibrations moving through my body.

Please tell me you just finished.

I smiled tiredly down at my phone on the armrest. Picking it up, I typed a reply.

Maybe. Did you?

Yeah, yeah I fucking did. Goddamn, we need to do that in person.

Calm down. We haven't even kissed yet.

I like the look of that 'yet'.

Don't get ahead of yourself, young man. That was a one-time thing.

Three magic dots, then came his reply.

Yeah right, Ells. We'll see about that.

I should've told him no, I meant it, this would never happen again. But it was a lie. After the pain Kayden had caused, it was good to feel sexual and desired, to be a woman instead of a punching bag and a slave and all the things my husband had made me.

Kayden was dead – he was fucking *dead* – and it was time I allowed myself a little happiness.

20

Blakelyn rang the next morning, my phone vibrating from beside the small notebook I sometimes jotted ideas in. But this morning there had been no ideas, my gaze fixated on the sea and the gathering silver clouds, my thoughts going over and over everything that had happened.

I snatched up my phone. 'Hello.'

'Ellie.' She sighed. 'We've had roughly fifty of the reviews removed. They were connected to new accounts, probably made just to leave the reviews. But the rest come from legitimate accounts, with review histories, and several of them are disputing the removals.'

'So what happens now?' I asked, unable to hide the anxiety in my voice.

'We're going to keep working at it. But it would be good if we knew why this was happening.'

A light rain was tapping against the window, and for far too long I watched the path the raindrops made down the glass. I had no desire to tell my publisher about my husband, about his mother, about any of this messiness.

I wanted to appear like what I aspired to be: a professional author.

'Ellie?'

'Yes, I'm here. Sorry. It's... the book is good, right, Blakelyn? What they're saying, these reviews, they're not right, are they?'

I hated how pathetic I sounded. I hadn't intended to ask the question, but it arose from some deep place inside of me, hungry for affirmation the same way I'd been as a girl at Mum's typewriter.

'Ellie, it's a fantastic book. But that won't matter much if we can't get these reviews sorted. If you can't tell me what's going on, I understand. But if you know who's behind this, I'd appreciate it if you tried to remedy the situation.'

'I'm not sure I can.' I reached up and swiped a bothersome tear from my cheek. 'I spoke to the person who's behind it, who I *think* is behind it. We didn't exactly end the conversation on good terms.'

There was a long pause. I was sure I could hear her grinding her teeth. 'That's not good. I won't lie to you. This could be very bad, and not just for this book.'

I didn't bother to ask what she meant, because I knew. Of course I knew. If this book performed poorly they wouldn't accept another from me. Because publishing was an artistic endeavour, people often forgot it was a business, and like any business they needed a return on their investment.

'We'll keep working on our end,' she went on. 'But please fix this. Whatever you have to do, however badly you have to grovel, it'll be worth it in the long run. I'm assuming this is a personal issue with somebody?'

'Yes. My mother-in-law.'

She laughed drily, sounding for a maddening second like Paisley, mocking me. I cautioned myself to calm down. That was the us-versus-them thinking that had led Mum to build intricate forts in the house, interwoven worlds of blankets, drawing the curtains against imagined invaders. 'Jesus, that's insane. Why would she possibly do this?'

It was my turn to laugh without a hint of humour. 'The truth? My estranged husband committed suicide...' *That's what you think*, Kayden whispered from my mind. *But I'm out there, waiting, watching.* I pushed on: 'And she blames me for it.'

'That's... I'm sorry, Ellie. Really. I take it you don't get along?'

'That's one way to put it.'

'It's going to be tough, but please try to make her stop. I've never seen anything like this before, all these reviews coming from one person. The new accounts make sense. She could've created those by herself. But the verified accounts?'

'Maybe she paid them.'

'She must have. It's fucked up, Ellie. It's really fucked up.'

'Agreed.'

'Please try and sort this.'

'I will. I'll try. But what if I can't? What happens then?'

'The book releases with those reviews. Not everybody reads reviews, so I'm sure you'll still move some copies. But it will definitely have an effect. We'd prefer for them to be gone.'

I would prefer that, too, of course, but I found it incredibly unlikely considering how Paisley and I had ended our call: the names I'd flung at her, the viciousness we'd exchanged.

It was much better instead to think about how mine and Freddy's text conversation had ended. After the sexting, we'd spent the next hour talking about everything and nothing, about music and books and films and silly jokes. It was nice to forget for a while, but I couldn't avoid my problems forever.

There was no way around it.

For the sake of my career, I was going to have to apologise to Paisley.

21

The voices were always there, whispering and taunting and encouraging and telling me to end my life. They rode the breeze and they crashed between my ears when I listened to music – even classical music without lyrics – and they buzzed on bees' wings and pitter-pattered in rainfall, always, always... except when I sat down at my typewriter. Then they would vanish, deserting me, and I'd be left with a blank page and a feeling of profound failure.

Except sometimes there was another voice, the worst of the wicked bunch. 'You really think you can write, you silly whore? You stupid mental bloody bitch. You really think anybody wants to read this drivel?'

The voice belonged to two hands, two vicious thick hands, which would tear up my pages and toss paper petals into the air.

I often wonder what sort of person I would've been had this peculiar illness left me alone. If I had lived in that cottage as a sane woman, with the inner will to clean myself and my surroundings up.

I was living in squalor and barely eating. Sometimes I would roam the woods and pick up mushrooms and berries and gobble them down like some medieval vagrant, and oftentimes this capricious gorging would make me ill.

But I had no choice, I thought, because going to the local shops was anathema to me. I felt sure every shopkeeper and villager and pedestrian and driver was out to get me, every laugh was directed at me, because they were trying to steal my book idea... my book which would change the world, and which I had not written a single page of.

Do you see how lacking in logic my mind was back then?

I had only avoided starving by living on the canned goods my parents had left in the cellar, many of them out of date. It was a tragic existence. I do not mean to pity myself. I have done too much bad in my life to indulge in that sort of behaviour, but I must state the facts as they were. I was living like an animal.

Kayden noticed how degraded I looked the next time we met. In our previous meeting we had wandered through the woods together, saying little, or at least *he* had said little as I told him about my friends, my characters in the foliage, the voices in the rustling leaves. I never usually felt comfortable speaking with such forwardness about my greatness – how I thought of it then – or my delusion: what I know it was now.

But Kayden was an attentive young man, never mocking or judging. In fact he had looked fascinated as I recounted my myriad madnesses.

So, the next time we met.

I had been returning to the tree to which he had tied his noose, in the hopes I would run into him again. It turned out he'd been doing the same, with the same hope. We met one blazing afternoon, Kayden emerging from the shadows of the trees with his shirt tucked into the waistband of his shorts, his torso extremely compelling. I hate to think of how I ogled him, and more so of how I skipped over to him and ran my grimy fingernail between his pectorals and down his hard belly muscles.

I was filthy. The fact he did not cringe away should have been a warning sign. But it was not.

'When's the last time you ate, Lottie?' he said to me.

I told him it had been a couple of days.

'I can tell. You look very thin. Where are you staying? I'll bring you something to eat.'

I told him the address of the cottage, and he told me that he'd heard about the crazy lady living up there, the lady who never opened her curtains. We laughed together about this.

Kayden said, 'Fuck them. I'd rather be crazy than boring.'

I laughed and draped myself over him, bringing my lips close to his ear. I must've reeked to high heaven, but somehow he didn't cringe away. He looped his arms around me and we held each other. He smiled, and I'm ashamed to say I loved the way he smiled, the way his gaze seemed to utterly consume me, as though my delusions were being proven true by the curve of his lips.

I asked him why he wouldn't kiss me. 'Because I can't kiss you first,' I explained.

'I've never kissed a woman before.' For a second he looked terribly young. Terribly young. 'Not really. I've been kissed. But I've never properly kissed anyone. That doesn't make sense, does it?'

It made complete sense to me, for I had read his mind: I had seen his mother climbing atop him, her podgy hand stroking him between the legs, as he croaked and sobbed and didn't ask her to stop. He had long since abandoned believing it would end, any of it would end, and so he lay there, dead-eyed, so dead-eyed and hollow and shattered and he stared at the ceiling, he stared and the bed whined like a dying animal and that woman wheezed and brought her lips close to her son's and kissed him tenderly as she finished, whispering in his ear that it was *his* turn to finish.

I know the monster he became: the pain he inflicted on my daughter. And yet I still pity him for what he endured. Does that make me a traitor to sweet Eleanor?

'How old are you?' I asked him, and he said to me, 'Eighteen, I'm eighteen.'

'That's too old to never have kissed anyone.'

'Okay...'

'I'm a lady,' I said. Which was a very silly thing for me to say, with my crusty hair and my unwashed body and my grime-encrusted fingernails. 'And a lady doesn't make the first move.'

He took a bolstering sort of breath then. That should've been another sign. Then he smiled and he leaned close to me. I felt his breath move through me, and for a moment I felt sure it was going to expand and explode and I would splatter the trees in my blood. And far from fearing this outcome, I longed for it. I leaned closer to make it more probable.

Our lips touched. We kissed.

The kiss deepened, and I was doomed.

22

I pushed the door to my flat open and hurried inside, slamming it behind me, eager for the day to be over. There had been more poor reviews, more tongue-lashing from Nigel, more stress. The only solace had been Freddy swaggering around the office, aiming smirks at me that had my insides swirling. I found myself feeling surprisingly shy, considering what we'd done via text, the heat we'd shared.

I still had to ring Paisley and apologise.

I'd told myself I was going to do it at lunchtime, and then my afternoon break, but I kept putting it off, giving myself an hour's reprieve, until an hour had turned into an entire day and there I was.

I took out my mobile and stared down at her number. This was going to be absolutely insufferable, but I'd wanted to be a writer for as long as I could remember. What had started as a bizarre exercise in madness – for Mum's benefit – had become a smouldering passion that had always seemed out of reach.

I had to say sorry. It was a simple word. I didn't have to mean it.

I pressed *call* and walked around the flat, into my office

where the curtains were still shut. Sunlight glowed through them, turning the room a copper shade.

I needed to get some blackout curtains.

Complete darkness: a perfect place to hide from Kayden's phantom.

'Hello?' Paisley grunted. 'Yes, Paisley Hunter speaking.'

She had an old-fashioned landline, without caller ID. I almost hung up, taking my chance, letting her assume it had been a mistaken call. But I had to do this.

'It's me. Ellie. I'm calling to apologise.'

I dropped into my desk chair and picked at the leather arm with my free hand. The material was scarred and flaky from where I'd stabbed at it before. I curled a piece between my fingers and let it drop to the floor.

She was indulging in an overlong pause. I had no choice but to wait.

'Go on then. Apologise.'

My instinct was to say, *I just did*. But that wouldn't get me anywhere.

'I'm sorry. For the way I spoke to you. For disrespecting you.' I hoped my voice sounded more sincere than I felt. 'I don't think Kayden would want us to fight. Whatever else is true about him, he loved us both.'

Lies, lies, lies... but if I had to say Kayden was the most honourable man in the world to get her to leave my book alone, I would.

'Very nicely said. But I'm afraid I don't accept.'

I bit down. My teeth hurt. I bit down some more. 'Why not?'

'Oh, there are lots of reasons, you silly girl. Things you could never guess. Things you wouldn't believe.'

'What the fuck does that mean?' So much for being civil. My voice flared. 'You're not making any sense.'

'Not once did you say you were sorry for my son's death.

Blah-blah-blah, sorry for this and that, but what about my sweet Kayden's suicide... any opinion?'

'I–'

A gunshot went off. The window smashed and the curtains fluttered.

A hand grenade tumbled into the room.

I screamed and leapt to my feet, dropping my phone.

Shards of glass were everywhere.

No: not a grenade, of course not a grenade. A brick. It sat amidst a bed of glittering glass.

Somebody had thrown a fucking brick through my window.

Without thinking, I spun and made for the door.

This had gone far enough. This was simply too much. I couldn't take this shit lying down anymore.

I threw open the door, ran down the hallway, burst onto the street.

A man was running toward the end of the road, wearing a black jumper with the hood pulled up, black trousers, chunky black combat boots.

I knew it was stupid. As I ducked my head and sprinted after him, I knew I was making a mistake.

23

I ran as fast as my legs would carry me, cursing my unused gym membership and my nightly glasses of rosé as my legs burned and my chest got tight. But I was fuelled by rage; powerful, all-consuming.

I kept running.

The man – at least I assumed he was a man, since he was tall and wide-shouldered – ducked around the corner and ran toward the entrance to the nearby park.

'Stop!' I yelled idiotically. What the hell did I think I was going to do if he *did* stop? 'Fucking *stop.*'

He kicked open the park gate, whining on its hinges, still swinging back and forth by the time I reached it. Though it was still bright and the evening was warm, this park wasn't central to the town and it was up a steep hill, so it was dead quiet despite the weather.

I grabbed the gate and threw it open, standing with my hands on my hips, looking from the children's play area to the pond to the small copse of trees. The public toilets were off to my left, reeking of piss, and I wondered if he was hiding in them.

I walked around the building. The doors to the toilets were

locked and required twenty pence to access them. I didn't have any change on me, but maybe the brick-thrower did? I circled the rest of it, checking behind, but it was clear he'd gone, whoever he was.

I walked through the park, urging myself to turn and go home.

The fucking *prick*.

What if I'd been standing next to the window? The brick could've struck me in the face, done me serious harm.

I thought about the figure in black, his hood pulled up, the shape of his body and the motion of his gait. I knew I had to stop letting my mind skip off to unhelpful places, but I couldn't ignore the notion it was Kayden. He'd been around the same height, the same width, the same everything. Though Kayden was older than me, he was fit for his age – vain like any narcissist – and he easily would've been able to outrun me.

I wandered through the park, over to the pond, standing at the edge and willing myself to calm down. The water held the sunlight, bouncing and shifting. I tried to study that instead of my paranoia, instead of allowing myself to think about how Kayden had returned from the dead – or he'd never died to begin with – and he'd decided to ramp up his torture.

The other stuff, the reviews and the callers, I found it difficult to imagine Kayden stooping to such petty things. *This* was definitely his style though. Sudden violence, unpredictable physical assaults, it was him all over.

The first mistake I'd made was chasing the man.

The second was standing at the edge of the pond when he was still most likely in the park.

What the fuck was wrong with me?

I turned at the sound of his footsteps, gleaming eyes staring behind a hockey mask, filled with glee and sadism and excitement. I felt sure they were Kayden's eyes, for half a second, maybe less. I was convinced.

But it happened so fast, his hands pumping out, slamming against my chest and sending me hurtling backward.

I screamed and my back met with water.

24

I hauled myself onto the water's edge, spluttering big mouthfuls of pond filth, the taste of it acidic and making my belly cramp. Bile followed the water as I clambered up on my hands and knees, crawling as far away from the pond as possible.

I knew I had to regain my composure quickly.

Kayden – or whoever this was – could return any moment.

I forced myself to look through blurry eyes around the park, knowing a swift kick could crunch into my ribcage any moment, the same way he'd kicked me dozens of times before: casually, as though kicking a woman in the stomach was the most natural thing in the world. My skin tingled in anticipation of a hand coiling around my neck, dragging me to my feet, his groin pressed against me as he whispered sick untruths in my ear.

But the park was empty.

I stood, breathing made difficult by the tightness in my chest. His hands had left painful imprints on my skin, my ribcage throbbing with the force of the impact. He'd attacked me confidently, savagely, the same way Kayden had over the years.

I left a dripping trail of pond water behind me as I trudged wetly out of the park, glancing behind me every few moments to make sure the attacker wasn't following. Tears stung in my eyes and sobs cracked in my throat. I tried to fight them; I told myself my crying years were behind me.

I ducked my gaze when a lady stopped on the other side of the road, glancing at me like she'd be willing to offer help.

Maybe she was in on it. Maybe the man in the hockey mask – Kayden or whoever the fuck he was – had hired her and she was going to lure me someplace he could torture me some more. I couldn't risk it.

I forced my mind to confront the practicalities of the next few hours.

I would have to ring the police and give them a statement. I'd need to board up my window and remove my valuables from my office, locking the door to the rest of the flat, and then contact my landlord to arrange the glass to be replaced. And I'd need to find someplace to stay.

I knew Georgia would happily let me crash on her sofa. She'd probably offer me her bed, kicking her husband out and sleeping on the floor. But she had children, a family, a life. I wouldn't impose.

It would be better to stay with Mum until the window was replaced.

But even with a new window, would I ever feel safe in my flat again?

First Kayden's face staring at me, now this.

I dreaded to think about what came next.

25

The sun had long since set when I climbed from the taxi, shouldered my bag, and walked up the lane to Mum's house. I hadn't told her why I needed to stay beyond the fact somebody had vandalised my flat.

I hadn't mentioned Kayden or the pond or the reviews or any of it.

I wasn't sure why. Perhaps I thought if I ignored it, I could pretend it wasn't happening.

I'd spent the last few hours talking with the police and my landlord, giving my statement and making arrangements to have my window replaced.

My landlord, while mostly a decent-seeming man, was a cost-cutter and had mentioned he *knew a bloke* who could help him fix this. He'd implied it might take a while, which bothered me, and hinted I could always sort it out myself.

The police had said they would follow up on the assault. They seemed like they were taking it seriously. But the officers had also mentioned that, without witnesses and CCTV, it would be difficult to find this man unless he'd done similar things to other people in the area. They'd asked me if I had any idea who it could be. I'd said no, I had no clue, because saying *yes, it was my dead husband* seemed too absurd.

But these were concerns for the next day. That evening all I wanted was to collapse and forget any of this had happened.

Mum walked onto the porch, wearing denim dungarees and an earth-stained shirt. Her bandana was lilac and her reassuring smile was tight, as though there was something lurking behind it. But that could've been paranoia playing tricks on me.

'Oh, Eleanor.' She pulled me into a hug, wrapping her arms tightly around my shoulders and squeezing me close. 'I'm sorry. I can't believe anybody would do this.'

We stayed like that for a time, her hand on my neck, stroking softly. I began to sob, hating the jagged sound of my pain even as I gave myself to it, as I buried my face in my mother's shoulder. She murmured soft, reassuring words, and then smoothed her hands down my shoulders and took a step back.

'How about some tea, hmm? Doesn't tea always make things better?'

'Sure. That sounds nice.'

I placed my bag on the kitchen table and sat down, resisting the urge to pick at the glossy veneer. She'd bought it at a charity shop and had spent several weeks restoring it, covering it in swirling intricate patterns. It was the sort of thing she never would have had the attention span to pursue when she was ill, and normally the sight of it heartened me.

But that evening all I felt was dread, bone-deep fear.

I pictured the eyes within the hockey mask, the way they'd beamed at me, pleased with what he was about to do.

I couldn't remember the colour: if they'd been Kayden's bright blue. It had happened too fast.

Mum brought the tea and sat next to me, reaching over and squeezing my hand softly. 'I'm sorry, Ellie. I'm... I'm so sorry.'

'It's not your fault.' I moved the finger of my free hand

around the rim of my mug, over and over, as if by focusing on the heat and the motion I didn't have to think about Paisley and the rest of it. 'It's one of those things, I guess.'

Things you could never guess. Things you wouldn't believe.

That's what Paisley had said to me on the phone, before the brick, before the chase.

I had no clue what she meant.

'It's awful. I wish I could turn back time, make it so it didn't happen.'

'You're acting like you threw the brick.' There was unfair viciousness in my voice. She was reminding me of when I was a girl and, whatever happened, she'd find a way to reroute it back to herself. 'The window will be replaced and it'll be like it never happened.'

'But you've been through so much...'

I wasn't sure if she was talking about my childhood, the missing year in my memory, or my marriage to Kayden. But it didn't matter. It was too painful to talk about any of it, to *think* about any of it.

'Do you have anything stronger here? Some wine, maybe?'

'I don't keep alcohol in the house.'

'Oh.'

'It interferes with my medication.'

'Yes, I remember.'

She let go of my hand and drummed her fingernails against the table. 'But I can always run down to the garage? It's only a short walk.'

'No, I'm fine. I'll drink this and try and get some sleep. It's been a long day.'

I took a sip of the tea, ignoring the fact it was too hot, scalding my tongue. Focusing on the burning heat was better than the tightness in my chest, the thoughts flurrying around my mind.

The eyes in the hockey mask: the maybe-Kayden eyes, staring, savouring, planning.

26

Mum hadn't preserved my bedroom the same way some parents did. The year after I moved out – taking my first admin job in Bristol, which would lead to years of flitting between jobs and partying and generally being young and achieving little – she'd turned it into a guest room. Sometimes her friends would sleep over, ladies she'd met at bingo and through the local gardening club, but that evening it was empty.

Dropping onto the bed, I stared at the ceiling, replaying the shove over and over. My skin felt too sensitive, my clothes rough. I didn't want to strip down in case I had to make a run for it: in case the man in the hockey mask returned.

I tried to sleep for a long time, changing position, closing my eyes and then opening them. Hours passed in this way, as I lingered in that state between rest and wakefulness, neither alert enough to spring out of bed nor comfortable enough to sink into a deep rest.

Finally I climbed out of bed and made for the door.

I'd make myself a strong coffee, sit myself at the table with my laptop open, and *drag* some words out of me if I had to.

I opened the door quietly and crept down the stairs, hoping I didn't wake Mum.

But she was already awake, sitting at the dining table, her head buried in her hands with a mountain of letters laid out before her. There were so many, they sprawled across the table, dozens and dozens of them.

Overdue, I read on one envelope. *Urgent. Late. Final notice.*

She spun, staring wide-eyed at me, looking like the mother from my childhood.

These were bills, overdue bills, but Mum was extremely wealthy from the money her parents had left her. She'd never flaunted it, but I'd always known she had enough to live the rest of her life comfortably... and for *me* to live the rest of my life comfortably if I'd taken her up on the offer.

Where had her money gone?

'Mum, I don't understand. What's happening?'

27

'Will you give me a moment?' She hastily began to gather the letters up, but it was an impossible task when she'd spread them so widely across the table. She ended up pushing several of them to the floor in her efforts. I knelt and picked one up. '*Eleanor.*'

I ignored her and scanned the letter, my eyes flitting over the lines: lines that told me Mum was several weeks behind on her electricity bill and she needed to rectify this immediately. My mind whirred, trying to figure out what she had possibly spent her money on. She didn't live an extravagant lifestyle.

She leapt up and snatched the letter from me, her hand trembling as she replaced it on the table. 'I asked for a moment. This is my house. Respect my wishes.'

'I don't understand. Why aren't you paying your bills?'

'I'm sorry, but that's none of your business.'

'You have the money. Don't you? Mum, you have the money?'

'That is *none of your business*.' Her hair was down, not tied up with a bandana as it often was, so it fell in tangled waves to her shoulders as though she'd been running her hands through it.

She seemed older than usual, somehow, as though the stress had aged her. Her lip curled and she pointed her finger at me. 'How many times do I have to ask you?'

'Mum, if I give you a second to clear away these bills, and then come back in here, that doesn't erase them from my mind.'

'Please don't get sarcastic with me.'

'Then explain what the fuck is going on.'

She threw her hands up, turning to address an imaginary crowd. 'Oh, she's swearing at her own mother. How delightful.'

I forced myself to slow down. I knew I was too close to the edge, primed from all that had happened the past week, ready for a fight. And even if Mum didn't deserve my rage, I knew I could too easily aim it at her. 'I'm sorry for swearing. But surely you can see how this would be a bit of a shock for me. I thought you were okay for money, with your inheritance.'

'*Your* inheritance, you mean.' The old meanness returned to her eyes, reminding me of innumerable times she'd directed the same glinting cruelty at me. 'Please don't pretend this is about me.'

'I've never taken your money.' I cautioned myself to lower my voice, to stay calm. But my next words came out ragged and far too loud. 'I've never asked for your fucking money. And that's a good point. You're always offering to help me. Just last week, you said you'd help me quit my job if I wanted to. Why would you say that if you didn't have the money? But if you have it, why haven't you paid your bills?'

'That is none–'

'I'm your daughter, the only family you have, and you're the only family *I* have. How can you look me in the eye and say this is none of my business?'

She floundered, her mouth opening and closing. 'Please, Ellie. Just... please.'

'Please what? *Where has your money gone?*'

It wasn't the money itself, but the fact she was flatly refusing to share something with me. Despite what we'd been through together – my father's death and all that had come after – we'd always been close. Even when she was torturing me with her psychosis, we'd found common ground through a shared love of writing, we'd always hugged and told each other *I love you*. We'd never kept secrets, at least as far as I knew.

But it seemed I didn't know much at all.

'Don't shout at me. You have no right to shout at me.'

'So you're not going to tell me?'

'I can't.' She started gathering up the letters, slower this time, as her hands continued to quiver. 'It's my problem, not yours.'

'Is it a man? Mum? Did you meet a man and he's been taking your money?'

She pulled a wicker box from one of the dining chairs and placed it on the table, methodically placing the letters inside as though they were precious gemstones. 'I'm sorry, but I'm not going to indulge in this any longer. I think it's extremely unfair. This is my home and if I don't wish to discuss this, you shouldn't try to force me.'

I knew she was probably right. I should've respected her wishes. But I wasn't some superhuman paragon of virtue, and I'd challenge any daughter to simply leave something of this magnitude alone. I'd arrived at the house to a mother who was wealthy, had always been wealthy, and now she was on the verge of losing her home. And she wouldn't even tell me *why*.

Maybe that's why I snapped. The shock of the fall.

'You shouldn't have cut your legs into fucking ribbons and forced me to mop up the blood. You shouldn't have told me you'd disown me if I rang an ambulance for you. You shouldn't have called me a slut when you found me and Theo kissing in the garden when we were kids. There's lots *you* shouldn't have done, but do I ever bring it up? *Ever?* And you won't have the decency to tell me the truth.'

She'd been placing her letters into the box as I ranted, but finally she spun, pushing the box to the floor. The letters spilled out and her face bloomed crimson. 'How dare you throw that in my face. I was a sick woman. I was...'

So many excuses, all the time, so many retreats from what she'd done.

'Where. Is. Your. Fucking. Money?'

'You vicious girl. What's wrong with you? It's *my* money. If I want to give it away to charity, or burn it, or do anything else with it, I will. Because it's *mine.*'

'I'm not saying I deserve any of it. I just don't understand why you won't tell me where it is, what's happened, anything. It's not fair.'

'Fair? Listen to yourself. You sound like a child.'

'As if you'd remember how I sounded as a child. You mad bitch.'

I hated the words the moment I'd spoken them. I almost wrapped my arms around her and told her I loved her. I was sorry.

But then she stepped forward, with reflected anger in her eyes, and prodded me in the chest. I gasped in pain. She'd hit me exactly where the man had, my skin still sensitive. '*I'm* the mad one? Ha! I should've left you to rot in that mental hospital. But you still don't know why you were there, do you? Say what you want about me, girl, but I've never lost a whole year of my life.'

I raised my hand and brought it down, close, so close to her face.

I stopped at the last moment, sickened by her words, by the truth of them.

But that didn't mean I had to stay here to listen to her.

I paced from the room, marching up the stairs.

'Eleanor,' she called from the bottom. 'I'm sorry. I shouldn't have said that.'

I hadn't unpacked my bag. I grabbed it and stomped down the stairs, ignoring her repeated apologies.

I spun when I reached the front door, glaring at her. 'Tell me what happened with your bills and I'll stay.'

Tears stung in my eyes. There I was, acting weak again: prey, the sort of woman silver-haired narcissists targeted and tortured. I wanted to be strong and capable, one of those kick-ass heroines from the fantasy novels I sometimes read.

'I can't.' She straightened her shoulders. 'But please don't go.'

I grabbed the handle and wrenched the door open. The street was pitch-dark from where the council turned off the street lamps. It had gone two in the morning. I cringed to think of the neighbours hearing our screaming match.

'Eleanor...'

I marched down the pathway, promising myself I wouldn't break down until I was well out of sight and earshot. I walked quickly, my throat getting tight, my belly churning.

Finally, when I rounded the corner at the end of the street, I collapsed against a lamp post and let out a jagged sob. The tears came hotly, streaming down my cheeks, as I replayed her words over and over in my mind: the same way I'd replayed the reviews and Kayden's insults and every bad thing ever flung at me.

She was right. That was the worst part. Losing a year of one's life was not normal.

But that didn't mean she had to throw it in my face. *I* was the one who supported her through my childhood, who lied for her, who kept her out of mental hospital. I was the one who'd protected her, when it should have been the other way around.

I forced my tears away and kept walking.

I'd go home and lock the door to my office, hoping the hockey-mask man or anybody else didn't kick in the boarded-up window and charge into my bedroom, hoping I could hold on for a little longer.

28

If my life was a film, when I sat down at my desk the next morning Georgia would've arched her eyebrow and said, 'You look like shit. Did you sleep at *all* last night?' And then she'd make me tell her everything that had happened, drawing it out of me as Hollywood best friends do.

But in real life sleeplessness can be hidden with artfully applied make-up, and most of the time people are too concerned with their own lives to pay attention to stuff like that.

I dropped into my chair, my body aching from tiredness and last night's assault. I'd had a short phone call with the police this morning, the officer asking if I was okay, if I was safe. I'd told them yes if I felt anything but.

Staying in the flat had turned me into the Ellie who flinched at every noise, every night-time creak, when I was married to Kayden. The house's settling had become a thousand stealthy intruders, each of them ready to finish what the hockey-mask man had started.

I was only in work because I needed this job, doubly so now I didn't have Mum's safety net to fall into. Nigel was a real pain in the arse when it came to taking sick days.

'Morning, hon.' Georgia looked up from her phone, her thumbs still typing furiously. 'Get any writing done last night?'

'Some,' I lied. Which was a mistake. I'd lied to her about Kayden and had promised never to do so again, and yet I wasn't sure how to lay it out there. It was too tangled and messy. I'd thought hard about where Mum's money had disappeared to, and come up with nothing. 'What about you? Did you have a nice evening?'

She told me a story about her husband pretending to enjoy her curry, the laughs they'd shared when she called him out on it, the stealthy sex they'd had afterward. 'I swear to God, having children seems like a great idea until you want to get your freak on.'

I laughed in all the right places, but I didn't feel present at all. I was watching everything unfold from a small box at the back of my head, the same way I had whenever Kayden let his devil out.

I was about to log in to the system when Nigel did his wannabe-soldier routine and marched across the office, his arms behind his back and a stern look on his face. 'Ellie, I need to have a word.'

'Anybody would think you had a crush on her, Nige.' Georgia flashed a smirk at him. 'Seriously, why not let her get on with her work?'

Nigel glared. 'Don't push your luck, Georgia. Ellie, my office.'

Georgia rolled her eyes, aiming her middle finger at him when he spun and walked away. I sighed and rose to my feet, following him, dragging my body across the office, everything sore and tired.

The moment I'd closed the door to Nigel's office, he laid his hands on the table and leaned forward. 'I need you to take a few weeks off until I can sort out this review business. There have been several more. We really can't have this. I've spoken to my superiors and they agree.'

'Paid?' I asked, which was probably not the most tactful thing to say. But I wasn't in the mood for tact. If he was going to pay me to leave this place, I'd sprint for the door.

'We have agreed you can take it as sickness. It will be statutory pay.'

I walked over to the desk, heat pumping through me. Statutory pay would hardly cover my rent. I had a small amount in savings, but not enough that I could wilfully throw it away. 'Nigel, I haven't done anything wrong. Those reviews were added by the same person. This isn't fair.'

'Fair or not, it's the best route for the company. Hopefully we can get this sorted and you'll be back in a few days' time.'

'But I can't live on statutory pay. And you can't force me. Legally you can't force me to take the absence as sickness.'

My heart was thumping far too heavily in my chest. I felt like I was going to burst pathetically into tears. I despised the feeling, hated feeling weak and easily stirred to emotion. But it had been a tough few days, and this was only making it worse.

'No,' he said after a pause. 'But there are provisions in your employment contract relating to the company's public image. If we feel it's necessary, we can use those as a basis for a disciplinary meeting and...'

'And fire me. You'd fire me for something I didn't do.'

I thought perhaps there was a glint of something in his eye, regret maybe, but I could've been imagining it. Mostly he was ice. 'If we had to, yes. Because if we don't, everybody here is in danger of losing their jobs, not being able to pay their mortgages and support their kids.'

I turned my face away, so he wouldn't see the tears rising in my eyes. 'Perhaps legally you can do this. But how the fuck are you going to justify it to yourself?'

'Ellie, don't swear at me.'

'But how?' I demanded. 'You *know* those reviews aren't from genuine customers.'

'Do I?'

'Yes.' I pawed at my cheeks, leaned over the desk, forced my gaze to return to his. 'It doesn't make sense. All this time working here, and nobody's ever left a negative review where I'm specifically mentioned. And then – after *one* incident – dozens start flooding in? It doesn't make sense.'

'We can't have an employee here who reflects poorly on the company. In your contract it stipulates you make every effort to ensure this doesn't happen.'

'I have made every effort.'

'No, no you have not. Because those reviews are still up.'

I almost groaned, screamed, kicked the fucking desk.

How could I explain to him about Paisley, about how utterly impossible she was to negotiate with? How could I explain to him about the way Kayden had torn up my insides over and over, so I'd gotten used to the sight of blood in my piss? How could I explain about the hateful way my heart would light up every time he smiled, because it meant he might not hurt me that evening?

'I need this job. If I have to take it as sickness, at least give me full pay.'

'I can't do that. We're not doing well as it is.'

'How am I supposed to sort the reviews if I can't pay my bloody rent, Nigel?'

He massaged the bridge of his eyebrows. 'I get that you're not happy about this, but it's what we've decided. You're welcome to seek legal assistance if you think that's necessary. But I should warn you, we've vetted this plan completely. You don't have a leg to stand on as long as those reviews are still up. I'm sorry.'

'Are you? Are you sorry?' I hissed. 'I don't think you're

capable. In fact, I think there's another reason you don't want me around here. Maybe you want to fuck me. Or maybe you're a sick bastard who gets his kicks by upsetting women. Yes, maybe that's it...'

My voice was rising, far too loud, far too vicious, the same way I'd shouted at Mum.

'I will *not* be spoken to like this.' He leapt to his feet, causing me to jolt back as electric instinct purged me of my bravery.

Any time a man moved erratically, a fist, a shoe, a kiss might follow... and now I was back there, strapped to the bed, staring wide-eyed as Kayden loomed over me, one hand stroking.

Nigel paused, as though realising the effect he was having on me. Perhaps there was some humanity in him after all. 'Go home. Get some rest. And get those reviews taken down. That's all you can do.'

'Maybe.' I turned away and made for the door. 'Or maybe I'll hire a lawyer. See how ironclad this contract really is.'

'I wouldn't advise it,' he called after me. 'You'd only be wasting your money.'

I left the office and took a sharp left, making for the toilets. I managed to keep myself together until I pushed my way inside. The moment I knew I was alone, I ran into one of the stalls and dropped onto the toilet seat, burying my face in my hands and sobbing.

I fought the crying even as I collapsed into it, as it wrecked me. I knew it didn't help a damn thing. But I couldn't stop.

The pervert customers, Kayden's face leering in the glass, the homeless man on the beach, my book reviews, the *work* reviews, the hockey-mask man and the brick and the cold pond water rushing around me... Mum and her secrets, secrets I'd never dreamed she'd keep from me.

'Ellie?' Georgia was outside the stall. 'Can I come in?'

I cleared my throat. 'Yes.'

'Oh, Ellie. What happened?' She knelt down and smoothed her thumb over my cheek, the same way she had when we were kids and I'd had a falling out with Theo. 'What did he say?'

I told her quickly.

Her features grew grimmer the more I spoke, until she sprung up and slammed her hand against the wall. 'That piece of *shit*. It's not your fault some losers have decided to leave those reviews. I'm going to speak to him.'

'No, Gee.' I stood and touched her wrist. 'You need this job. Come on. You know what he's like. He'll make your life hell if you take a stand on this.'

I couldn't put her family at risk: her husband, her kids, her normal, happy, beautiful life.

'It's such bollocks.' She folded her arms.

'Yeah, but that's life.'

'Well, it shouldn't be.'

I laughed drily. 'I'm not going to argue with you on that one.'

29

I left the office once I'd wiped the last of my tears from my cheeks, walking down the cobblestone pathway toward the main road. Then I heard footsteps behind me, running loudly on the stones, and I turned, certain he was back, but this time he'd do more than push me into a pond.

Freddy stopped and stared. For a second I thought he was angry at me. His features were twisted and his eyes blazed. 'Georgia just told me what happened. Fuck, Ells. That's out of order.'

I shrugged, finding it difficult to meet his gaze. That was how I knew I really liked him. Despite everything, I was acutely aware of how tired I must've looked, especially since my crying had ruined my make-up. 'I can't do anything about it. It doesn't matter.'

'*I* can do something about it. Wait here. I won't be long.'

'Freddy, you can't...'

But he'd already spun and made toward the office. He threw open the glass door so aggressively I was surprised it didn't smash.

I had no idea what he could say, but Freddy did seem to have a strange relationship with Nigel: getting away with more than any of us. He'd saved me from that tongue-lashing, but I doubted he could help me with this.

I sat on the wall, kicking my legs, feeling like a teenager waiting for her boyfriend... waiting for Theo. He'd had a wall outside his house and I'd often sit on it while he got ready, and then he'd emerge with a cheeky smile on his freckly face, running his hand through his curly red hair. 'Sorry, Ells. But you know I have to look beautiful for you.'

I pushed thoughts of my childhood sweetheart away. They wouldn't help me. Plus they could lead to *that*.

Say what you want about me, girl, but I've never lost a whole year of my life.

'Ells.' Freddy swaggered over, grinning. 'Not sure if you'll be grateful or annoyed, but you're back in the game. Get your headset on and get ready to deal with self-entitled pricks.'

'Wait, what? Are you serious?'

He took a short bow. 'Come on. Don't act so surprised. I'd do anything for you.'

'But I don't understand. What did you say?'

'I told him I had a cousin who worked for a big newspaper, and if he pulled this shit he'd end up plastered all over the country as a bully and a sexist. That made him change his tune pretty damn quickly.'

I threw myself forward, flinging my arms over his shoulders before I had time to doubt myself out of the gesture. 'Thank you. You don't know how much this means to me.'

He smiled warmly, his hands casually resting on my hips, reminding me of our sexting session and the steaminess we'd exchanged. 'Let me take you out tonight. A few drinks, a few laughs. We can rant about what a prick Nigel is... and maybe, if you're very polite, I'll offer you a kiss.'

I slapped his chest playfully. 'You're a dick.'

'Is that a yes?'

The alternative was to go home to a flat which, if my landlord's lukewarm response had been anything to go by, was still vulnerable to any passing stranger in the street. Or maybe not a stranger: maybe Kayden in a hockey mask.

I knew I'd be safe with Freddy. I knew he'd protect me if anybody tried to hurt me again. It didn't once occur to me that Freddy might be the man in the mask.

'Yes. But you have to let me pay this time.'

He smirked. 'I can't promise that, Ells.'

30

I arrived at the bar early. The idea of skulking around the flat wasn't appealing to me, especially since my landlord had said it could take one or two more days to arrange to have the window fixed. I'd tried to argue with him over the phone, but I felt deflated from the previous night and that day, overtired and overstressed.

It was better to be in public, sipping a rosé as I watched people walk down the promenade, stifling the thought that somebody was going to run up behind me any second. I couldn't stop looking over my shoulder every time somebody walked by.

My gaze was drawn to a family of four. The mother was a young woman, probably in her mid-twenties, with a pixie cut of jet-black hair and a profoundly contented expression on her face. She pushed a pram, pausing to lean down and lay a tender kiss on her baby's forehead. The father and their toddler son rampaged ahead, the boy laughing as the man scooped him up.

I turned away quickly, stunned at the emotion which tried to choke me.

There was something so picture-perfect about it, something so *not mine*.

It was the sort of thing Kayden and I had spoken about in the early days. Lying in bed together, his fingers moving through my hair, he'd talk passionately about the life we'd build. 'We'll have two kids, and we'll each have our favourite. I'll take the lad to the rugby and you'll go shopping and do your girly stuff.' I'd giggled and told him he was a brute, no clue how right I was.

When I *did* finally get pregnant, I had to do the unthinkable, and I still hated myself for it. It was legal and it was acceptable and it was my choice, but every time my thoughts strayed to it, I prayed for another dose of amnesia.

If I could lose a year of my life, why couldn't I lose *that* too?

I took another sip of my wine, remembering how Kayden's face had twisted when I told him I was leaving him.

It had taken every shred of courage I possessed. But I had to. Because I couldn't have another abortion, and Kayden refused to use contraception. I was terrified if I started to use the pill he'd find it, which would lead to a whole new hell I couldn't stand to think about.

He'd walked right over to me, his powerful chest heaving, his stark azures burning. 'You're going to abandon me.'

'It isn't working. You must see that.'

'You fucking whore.'

'Please.'

I knew what would come next: what always came next.

But then he stepped back and this dead-cold look came into his face. After a moment, he'd smirked. 'All right, Ellie. Have it your way. But let me tell you, you're going to regret this. That's a promise.'

It was the threat that had made me so paranoid during the past year, sure Kayden was going to re-emerge violently into my life.

'Ells.' I looked up to find Freddy standing over the table. He was wearing a shirt with the top two buttons undone to show his chest. His smile was genuine and his eyes were kind. I hoped. Or he was tricking me: like Kayden had tricked me. 'Are you all right?'

He sat down and I nodded. 'I'm fine. Do you want a drink?'

'Sure, but I'll get it...'

'Nah-uh. It's my turn. What're you having?'

'If you insist, I'll take a beer.'

'I *do* insist. A beer it is.'

I had to focus on my footsteps as I made my way to the bar. The glass of wine had hit me far too hard. I leaned against the mahogany surface and smiled at the barmaid, a woman with dyed pink hair and a sleeve of colourful tattoos. 'We've got an offer on shots tonight,' she told me. 'Five for ten pounds. Any from the list.'

She gestured at a blackboard hanging over the bar, the alcohol written out in bold white chalk.

It would be a mistake, surely, to indulge in shots on no sleep and too much stress.

But I also knew it would make it much easier to push everything to the back of my mind. And after being targeted, insulted, *assaulted*, surely I was allowed to forget, at least for the evening.

I returned to the table balancing a tray heavy with my wine, his beer, and five shots of sambuca.

'Jesus, Ells. I thought you said a quiet one.'

'Are you complaining?'

He stood and took the tray from me, smiling in that captivating way of his: the way that urged me to reach over and run my fingers along his strong jawline. 'Not remotely. How we splitting these bad boys?'

'Because I'm nice, I'll let you have three.'

He picked up the shot glass, raising it in a toast. 'Here's to getting unnecessarily obliterated on a weekday.'

I laughed – it felt good, welcome – and picked up my glass. 'Cheers.'

I knocked it back, coughing as my eyes stung. He chuckled and picked up his second. 'You're not chickening out on me, are you, Ells?'

'Hell no.'

I knocked back the second and then gripped the edge of the table, leaning back and letting out a sharp breath. 'Damn, that really was unnecessary.'

He chuckled and then I was giggling, infecting each other with our laughter, our eyes meeting as we gave ourselves over to it. I wasn't sure what was so funny, but it didn't matter. It was enough that he could make me forget, make me live in the moment, despite the past and the future trying to split me apart.

If that didn't mean something, I wasn't sure anything did. I couldn't think of anybody else who could draw me out of my bad mood like this. It was like we were made for each other... which was an insane thing to think, and surely a result of the sambuca bubbling in my empty stomach.

We got more shots, and the night glittered and spun.

At one point I brought a glass to my eye, sighting him as though through a telescope. 'Tell me, young Frederick, why on earth are you not out with a nice young thing tonight?'

'A *nice young thing*? That sounded a bit weird.'

'Weird, how?'

He reached over and pinched my cheek. 'Weird like you're going to hunt down these *nice young things* – as you brand them – and chop them into pieces. Is that it? Are you a serial killer, Ells?'

I batted his hand away. 'It's true though. You could be out with...' A group of women were walking by, their hair sun-blonde and their skirts short, showing their athletic legs, their tanned skin. Everything about them was glamorous and sexy. I waved at them. 'With them! With one of them. But here you are with me.'

Freddy almost fell off his chair laughing when the women glanced over at me. Clearly I was making something of a scene.

My cheeks burned and I stared down at the table. 'Are they gone? Please tell me they're gone.'

'Yeah. But I think you made them a tad self-conscious.'

I glanced up to find they'd walked down the street. Shaking my head, I said, 'Maybe I need to keep my voice down.'

Freddy casually reached over and brushed my hair behind my ear, causing tingles to dance up and down my neck. 'Yeah, maybe.'

I reached up and took his hand, pressing it against my face. I was very drunk, but I didn't particularly care. 'That feels nice.'

He stroked his thumb along my cheek, my skin sizzling with the contact. 'When I first started at FCA, you were working on your book, right?'

'Yeah, well, I was working on the edits. I remember because Gee came to tell me one lunchtime that a hunk had started. You're lucky she's married or she would've had you for breakfast.'

'I would've still picked you. I'll always choose you.'

A warning siren blared within me. Kayden had said similar things. But his hand felt so *right* against my face. 'Cheesy.'

He shrugged. 'Maybe so. But also true. Anyway, I saw you one lunch break, sitting on the bench outside work with that notebook in your lap. You had this look on your face, Ells... it was...' He trailed off.

'What?' I urged.

'It was so focused, so in the moment, so completely dedicated to what you were working on. I remember the way you brushed your hair from your face. I remember the way you smiled when you got an idea, and how quickly you scrawled it on the page. I couldn't stop staring.'

My body felt warm at his words. 'Freddy.'

'Hmm?'

'I think maybe I'd like to go home.'

'That's cool. I'll ring you a taxi–'

'No.' I kept my eyes closed. Even with the alcohol, I couldn't say this as I gazed at him. 'I think maybe I'd like you to come with me.'

'Oh.' He paused, and then his voice rose. '*Oh...*'

'Yeah.'

Suddenly I felt his breath on my face.

I could smell the shots, the beer, but I didn't care. He was leaning across the table. I kept my eyes closed, firmly closed, and then his lips were on mine and I was moaning and he growled through the tight press of our mouths. Our tongues flared and went to war.

'Come on.' He stood and took my hand. 'We need to get out of here. Now.'

31

Our hands were greedy as we strode from the taxi toward my flat. I fumbled with the keys in the door and we both laughed. And we kept laughing. We couldn't stop. Then, once we'd slammed the door closed behind us, there was no room for laughter.

I leapt at him and wrapped my legs around his waist, gasping as he kissed my neck, as his hands got tight on my ass and everything became intense, important, vital.

There was no fumbling, no awkwardness.

Our bodies knew what to do and we gave ourselves over to the lust. We climaxed together, our eyes locked, lips close but not fused in a kiss. We painted each other in orgiastic breaths in those final moments.

Afterward, I lay in his arms, exhaustion catching up with me, as I felt his heartbeat slamming in his muscled chest. 'Will you stay here tonight, Freddy?' I murmured, already half asleep.

'Of course, Ells.' He kissed the top of my head. 'If I had my way, I'd never bloody leave.'

32

I have reached the part of my story I do not like to think about. I have spent the years following that summer purposefully putting this far back in my mind. First I consumed myself with getting better – with therapy and medication – and then, once I'd met my dear Zachary and we conceived Eleanor, I dedicated myself to my family. I often wonder what my life would've been like had cancer not cruelly struck my husband... or if, after his passing, I hadn't allowed myself to fall into a pit of despair.

I'd talked myself into believing my medication was dulling my grief, and I had to feel my grief if I was going to care for Ellie. I can see now this was my illness battering at the walls of the antipsychotics, desperate to be allowed back into my consciousness, but at the time the logic seemed trustworthy.

I've wished I could blot this summer from my memory ever since it happened, but if the mind will sometimes wipe away the past for a person – I know that far, far better than most – it turns out a woman cannot trigger it herself. Or, at the very least, *I* cannot trigger it.

I replay those moments over and over, hating myself with more bitterness with each recollection.

Kayden kept his promise to start bringing me food. Every day at around lunchtime, he'd stand at the end of my lane and wait for me to peer out of my window and see him. We'd arranged this after his first visit, when he'd knocked and sent me into a manic hunt for a hiding place.

I'd felt sure the knocking was *them*, whoever they were, the people: the endless people who were out to get me, who were going to kill me and rape me and steal my book idea, a book I hadn't written or started to write. It didn't matter if there was no logic in the fear.

He'd whistle twice. I still hear those whistles sometimes, like music that is far too welcoming, when I should remember them as sharp and ugly. Once I'd waved at him, he would swagger up the garden path with his hamper under his arm. More often than not he was shirtless. (Sometimes I saw the Other taking off his shirt.) He knew exactly what the sight of his bare torso did to me, and he was never surprised when I threw the door open and leapt at him.

I cannot say we made love, because that would not be strictly true.

We fucked. We fucked like rabid animals, as though fucking would bring us some sort of absolution.

Or, rather, *I* fucked like an animal.

For all his swagger and bluster, Kayden was very shy in the bedroom. He would lie back and stare up at me with his wide blue eyes, brimming with fascination, as I rode him as though my life depended on it: as I screamed as though I desired the whole world to hear how much I was enjoying it.

Sometimes, God, sometimes he would weep after we did this. He would bury his face in a pillow and weep, and what did I do, what was my response to these strange and incongruous tears? I would prance around the room munching on an apple or whatever else he'd brought me, ignoring the shivering lump in the corner of the room, ignoring the pain gushing out of him. And ignoring the Other, the pale shadow, who would sit in the opposite corner and watch it all: always watching, always there. Shimmering and fish-pale, this Other had become one of my most vivid hallucinations, and the mere sight of it caused vomit to broil inside of me.

In hindsight I can see why Kayden was crying. Of course, sex was a very confusing thing for him, tangled as it was amongst the abuse he'd received at the hands of his sick mother since he was a child. Again, I knew about this – I believed – because I had peered past his veneer to the fragmented boy beneath, exploring his memories and hate and pain: the first time she kissed him a little too long, the first time she held him a little too tightly.

I didn't question his tears, or the pale shimmering Other, or any of it. I pranced around and spoke of my book in half-formed sentences, gorging on the food he'd brought me, or sometimes, sometimes...

I hate myself.

If there is a reader of these words – if it's you, sweet Ellie, or anybody else – you have to know I despise myself. But I have to tell the truth. I can only exorcise these demons if I name them specifically, truthfully. Otherwise they will remain in my mind and continue their torture.

Sometimes, when Kayden was crying after our sex, I would go to him and lick the tears from his cheeks. I would lap them up and swallow them and grin in his face, telling him I was consuming his soul.

And didn't he like the idea of me consuming his soul? Didn't he like that?

As I spoke I would smooth my hand down his body. I'd grip his limp penis and I would stroke until it wasn't limp anymore. I saw in his eyes he didn't *want* to become erect, but he would, and then I would sit atop him and take what I thought was mine.

But it was only the sex that seemed to confuse him. Other times we would simply lie together, and the cheeky, confident Kayden would return. He'd move his fingers through my hair and, I hate to admit it, sometimes I still feel the sensation of his fingertips across my scalp, phantom remembrances.

Oh, how I detest myself.

'We could build a life together,' he said once. 'Me and you, Lottie. We really could. I think we're the only people alive who understand each other. You said it yourself. Everybody judges you. Everybody's out to get you. But not me. I'd never do anything to hurt you. I... I love you, Lottie.'

I sprung up and placed my hands on his chest. 'Say it again.'

We said it together, 'I love you, I love you, I love you.'

That became our favourite topic of conversation: this imagined life we'd start together. I would use my parents' money, and the fortune I'd undoubtedly get from my masterpiece (lunacy, just lunacy) and buy us a beautiful house far away from his parents. He was very forceful about getting as far away from his mother as possible. And always, when we lay together or spoke of our future, the ceaseless watcher would be absent, sinking away, drifting beneath the waves of the other voices and fledgling unrealities which populated my existence.

The plan was I'd spend my days writing and Kayden would have time to work out what direction he wanted to take his life. He was a young man, eighteen years of age, and he still had plenty of time to find his passion.

'Maybe I'm a painter,' he would say. 'Or a writer, like you. Or maybe I'm meant to be a builder or work in a shop. I don't care, Lottie, as long as we're together.'

I told him I didn't care either.

He was my Kayden. He was my dream man. He was the love of my life.

33

I woke to Freddy leaning up on his elbow, looking down at me with a soft smile on his face. His hair was ruffled and his eyes were the least sarcastic I'd ever seen them, brimming with something real, something significant. 'Morning, Ells.'

'What time is it?'

He grinned. 'Phew.'

'Few, a few what?'

'Not *few*, *phew*… as in, I'm relieved you're not awkwardly telling me to leave because last night was a mistake.'

I ignored the warning siren blaring in my mind and reached up, running my hand through his hair. 'Not every drunk sexual encounter is a mistake. And ours certainly wasn't. Unless you think so?'

'No damn way.' He leaned down and kissed the edge of my mouth. 'I wanted to know you felt the same. It's just gone seven, by the way. You've got plenty of time before work.'

I sat up, rubbing sleep from my eyes and leaning against the bedrest. Freddy shuffled up with me, putting his arm around my shoulder and hugging me close to him. I sighed contentedly and let my cheek rest on his shoulder. 'Hang on... you said *you've* got plenty of time. Me, not you. Are you not going into work?'

'Well, here's the thing. I got up to take a slash about an hour ago and I noticed a bunch of stuff piled up in the hallway. Now, being the curious bastard I am, I unlocked the door to your office – the key was in the lock, please don't be angry – and I saw the state of your window.'

'I'm not angry at all. But I don't see how that relates to you not going into work.'

'Obviously I'm going to be an absolute gentleman and get it sorted for you before you get home tonight. I mean, shit, Ells... anybody could break in here. What happened anyway?'

The hockey-mask man and the chase through the park felt too ugly to bring up now. It was poisoning what we'd shared: this beautiful thing we were beginning together.

Freddy's phone buzzed from the side table and he glanced at it. For a second, I was sure I detected anger in his eyes. Then he smiled and left me wondering if I'd imagined it.

'Aren't you going to check that?'

'Nah. It's probably a marketing email or something. I'd much rather enjoy my time with you.' He kissed the nape of my neck. Suspicion moved through me. Just like our first date, I wondered if it was another woman. But I didn't ask. I didn't have the energy for an argument, especially when I was probably being paranoid. He leaned up. 'Sorry. Got distracted there.'

My skin tingled from where he'd kissed me. 'No need to apologise for *that*. As for what happened to the window... it was kids, I guess.'

'Hmm.' Freddy nodded. I wasn't sure if he believed me, and I wasn't sure why I'd lied. 'Why hasn't it been fixed yet?'

'My landlord. You know how they can be.'

'Hey. That's racist to landlords.'

I laughed. 'Fine. *My* landlord is a selfish cheap prick. Better?'

'Much. Let me sort it for you. Go to work, endure that bullshit, and you'll come home to a brand-spanking-new window with your office clean and ready for you to write your next masterpiece.'

'Are you sure? What about work? Nigel will have your head on a stick if you don't give him a sick note.'

'Fuck Nigel. Fuck FCA. I don't care about that place.'

'Neither do I. But we all have to make a living.'

He shrugged, running a hand through his hair. For a terrifying moment he reminded me of Kayden.

Kayden had demonstrated the same cavalier attitude as far as money was concerned. During our marriage, he'd rarely worked, but he always had ready cash: from his past employments and the money from his dad's life insurance, he'd said, which he'd invested wisely when he was young. Despite his lack of employment, he was able to support us even when he wouldn't allow me to get a job. He'd still leave the house most days though, to go to the pub or a football match or the gym.

His lack of a job was one of the reasons it was difficult to navigate around him, because he'd appear at the most random moments, popping up when I started to get comfortable.

But Freddy wasn't Kayden. He was offering to do something nice, which by itself made him Kayden's utter opposite.

'So?' he said. 'Are you going to let me do this for you or not?'

'Obviously I'd prefer to have a window than a piece of cardboard. But Nigel really will freak if you don't show up.'

'Let him. I've got that prick in the palm of my hand.'

'How, Freddy? I don't get it. Did you and Nigel know each other before you started at FCA? Do you *have* something on him?'

'*Have* something?' He grunted out a laugh. 'Sorry, Ells. I didn't realise we were in a spy film. What could I possibly have on him?'

'Don't be a dick. I'm just saying. It doesn't make any sense. He's like a military drill sergeant with everybody else, but you seem to get away with murder.'

He smirked, bringing his face close to mine. The smell of him, the taste of him, the heat of him, it blotted everything else as we kissed, as we submerged ourselves in each other. And then we were gasping and exploring each other's bodies, desperate to be naked again, hungry to feel while sober what we'd experienced while intoxicated.

After the sex – after the soul-shattering orgasms – I found myself in a less inquisitive mood. And, anyway, I had to get ready for work. Freddy clearly wasn't going to tell me why Nigel had marked him out as a favourite, and maybe I was reading too much into it.

I should've asked more questions. Of course I should have.

'I feel like your stay-at-home husband,' he teased when I was stood at the door in my work clothes. I'd given him my only set of keys, relying on him being there when I returned home. I knew it could be a mistake but, even if it was mad, I trusted him. 'I'll have dinner waiting for you, honey.'

I laughed and we kissed again. I might've been wrong before. I still felt drunk, drunk on him. 'You better. Or there will be dire consequences.'

He chuckled and stepped back, snapping off a salute and then standing rigid with military posture. 'Yes, ma'am.'

'You really are a dick.'

'And you wouldn't have it any other way.'

'Annoyingly, you're probably right. Please don't burgle me. See you later.'

'I'm promising nothing,' he called after me.

I was smiling as I walked down the street. It was a stupid thing for me to do. I'd been assaulted and I was being targeted by Paisley... and possibly Kayden if she'd lied about his death.

An evening and a morning with Freddy shouldn't have been able to blot all of that.

I should've been cringing at every noise, made anxious by the tiniest movement at the edge of my vision.

And yet, miraculously, my smile remained fixed as I made my way to the bus stop.

Even if a dark look had come into Freddy's face when his phone vibrated: even if he wouldn't tell me why he got special treatment at work. Even if there were warning signs, clear and definitive warning signs, that I chose to ignore because he made me feel like a proper person again.

34

Work was, for once, not as terrible as it usually was. Or maybe it was the same and knowing I got to return to Freddy made it more bearable. Georgia gave me inquisitive looks all day, commenting once or twice that I seemed in a far better mood than I'd been lately.

I knew she was right, and I also knew it made no sense.

It could've been possible I was tougher than I gave myself credit for, that the hockey-mask man and the rest of it weren't enough to break me. But truthfully I knew it was the twenty-five-year-old from Wolverhampton, with his skin-fade haircut and his powerful hands.

I almost ran up the hill on my way home, wondering if I was going to return to a ransacked house. It would be another lesson not to trust men, one I should've learned the first time Kayden laid his hands on me.

But when I rounded the corner and saw the brand-new window glinting in the summer sunlight, I knew Freddy had kept his word.

I opened the door to my flat and immediately smelt flowers, their sweet scent lacing the air. The wall at the end of the hallway flickered with candlelight and rose petals were scattered over the floor, making a vivid red passage from the front door to the living room.

As I rounded the corner, my breath caught as I drank in the scene. He'd cleared away the sofa and folded out a small dining table, covered in more petals, with a bottle of champagne sitting in a bucket and dozens and dozens of candles burning everywhere, the light flickering.

Freddy was standing on the far side of the room, an acoustic guitar cradled to his chest, his fingers poised over the strings.

I let out a silly gasp, a romantic's gasp, the gasp of a woman who had fallen in love twice and been disappointed twice. And there I was, doing it all over again. 'Freddy,' I whispered.

He plucked at the strings and deep music filled the air. His fingers moved skilfully, his lips twisted into a captivating smirk. 'Dear Ellie, sweet Ellie, Ellie who is miiiiiine. Dear Ellie, sweet Ellie, for Ellie I'd give my liiiiiife.'

I dropped my work bag and my hands rose over my mouth. My heart was thumping hard.

'Dear Ellie, sweet Ellie, Ellie who is miiiiiine. Dear Ellie, sweet Ellie, for Ellie I'd give my liiiiiife.'

I blinked and tears flowed down my cheeks, his voice pitched low, deep and sweet-sounding at the same time. He wasn't a professional singer. There were quivers in his voice, notes of humanity, but that only made it more special.

'On a bench with the world in your eyes, one look at you and I'm paralysed. Hopeless, but when I saw dear Ellie, sweet Ellie, my hope began to riiiiiise. And now you're mine, dear Ellie, sweet Ellie, and our future's in the skiiiiies.' He grinned and strummed a couple more times. 'Sorry, Ells. That's as far as I got. Do you like it?'

I answered him by bursting into tears, emotion choking me, sobs making my throat tight and breathing difficult. I was crying too hard, too melodramatically, but he'd triggered something in me: something I thought had died years before.

Freddy laid his guitar on the table and paced across the room, pulling me into a hug. I pressed my face into his firm chest and wept, as his fingers moved through my hair and he whispered words I didn't hear, but their tone swirled through me. Their tone bolstered me, and after a few minutes I was able to look up into his confident eyes.

'That was amazing. Really amazing. You didn't have to do that.'

'I did.' He cradled my face, kissing the tears from my cheeks. 'You deserve to know how special you are. It's only been a little while with us – hell, hardly any time – but you can't tell me there isn't something special here. You can't tell me you don't feel it.'

'I feel it,' I told him passionately. 'I'm not sure how to explain it. But it's something, isn't it? It's real.'

'Oh, it's real, Ells. It's the realest thing I've ever experienced.'

We kissed for a long time, sinking into each other. And then he broke it off, but kept his face close to mine, so I could feel the shape of his smile against my lips. 'Come on.'

He took my hand and led me into my office.

I smiled giddily as my eyes moved over the room.

It had never looked this neat. My paperbacks had previously sat in a clumsy heap in the corner, but Freddy had installed a bookshelf on the wall and lined them up. He'd returned my desk and my computer and everything else to its rightful place. The new window shone and he'd fixed the curtain rail from where the brick had caused a few of the fastenings to come loose.

The only downside was the curtain being open, but I could hardly begrudge him that.

He didn't know about the face in the glass...

'Ellie. What is it? What's wrong?'

Freddy was facing me. He didn't see Kayden standing on the other end of the street. He had a broad smile on his face.

'He's there. Freddy. He's *right there*.'

'Who's where?'

I pointed. 'Look.'

Kayden darted away, disappearing from view, as Freddy turned around. 'I don't see anybody.'

'He was right fucking there,' I yelled, pacing over to the window. 'I'm not making this up. I'm not mad.'

'*Who* was there?'

'My husband, my dead fucking husband. But he can't be dead. He was staring at me.'

Freddy turned and frowned at me. There was a strange look in his eyes, as though he thought I was insane, as though he was debating how to tell me to calm down. I was ready to scream if he did.

A shimmering face in the glass was one thing, but it was still light outside, and I'd seen him in vivid detail.

There was no way my mind could conjure something so believable, was there?

'I'll go and check.' Freddy strode past me. 'Wait here.'

I stood at the window, waiting for Kayden to reappear. Freddy walked onto the street and out of view, returning a minute later and glancing at me with a shrug. I clenched my fist. This was a joke.

What was he doing, just *staring* at me?

It must've been him in the hockey mask.

But what if he was really dead? What if I was mad?

'Ellie, you need to explain what's going on,' Freddy said when he returned. 'I didn't know you were married. And if your husband's dead, how is he watching you? I don't understand.'

'You think I do?' I snapped.

He looped his arm around my shoulder and led me back

into the living room. The flickering candles, the roses, the champagne, it seemed out of place now, a relic from a different time.

Freddy sat me down at the table and seated himself opposite, staring hard. 'Tell me, Ellie. Whatever it is, we'll face it together.'

35

I told Freddy about all that had happened: the calls, the homeless man, the brick and the assault and everything, except for Mum's weirdness about her bills, because I couldn't see how that would relate to any of this. I told him about the face in the glass and how I wasn't certain if he'd truly been standing there, or if I'd let my mind play tricks on me.

'But you saw him.' He squeezed my hand, staring reassuringly. 'Just because I didn't turn around quickly enough, it doesn't mean you imagined him. I mean, hell. Have you ever had hallucinations before?'

'No. But there's precedent, I guess you could say, for my mind not exactly being reliable.'

'What do you mean?'

I took a large sip of champagne. It had seemed strange popping the cork in the middle of my rather macabre tale, but alcohol made all of this easier. 'You'll think I'm crazy if I tell you.'

Another squeeze of the hand, and he smiled. 'Try me.'

So I did. I told him about the missing year in my childhood, how I'd never allowed myself to question what had happened.

'Because if I do, I'll have to face it, whatever it is. And any time I get close, any time I *glance* there, I feel this… it's like my whole world's going to come crashing down. I know that sounds melodramatic. But it's also the only way I can think to describe it. I never let myself think about it.'

'Jesus.' Freddy sat back, shaking his head slowly. 'A whole year… and you have *no* idea what happened, why your mind, what, erased it?'

'Nope, none.' I laughed grimly. 'I told you. You think I'm crazy.'

He nodded. 'Yeah, maybe a bit.'

I found solace in his answer. He'd been honest with me when others would have immediately told me no, no, there was nothing wrong with me. But Freddy had told me the truth, how he really felt, and that held meaning. It meant he was trustworthy and reliable. That's what I thought.

'What are you thinking about?' I placed my glass down. 'Apart from the fact I'm completely bonkers.'

'I guess I'm trying to imagine what it would be like. So you woke up? From your point of view, I mean, that's how it felt?'

'Yes, I guess so. That's probably the best way to describe it.'

'So what's the last thing you remember?'

My mind jolted at his question, screaming to tell him to stay out of my business. Thinking about the last thing I remembered could all too easily lead to the rest of it, and yet I knew I was going to answer him. He was the first person I'd ever properly discussed this with. 'Theo's face, smiling at me.'

'Theo, as in your childhood sweetheart?'

'Yes, exactly. I remember him smiling at me. I think he had my hand in both of his, sort of cradling it, and he's talking very earnestly to me. He could be *so* serious for a teenage boy sometimes. He was extremely mature for his age.'

'What's he saying?'

'I can't hear the words. Just the tone. It's reassuring. Maybe he's trying to tell me everything's going to be okay, and then... *bang*. Mum's asking me if I can hear her. Apparently after the *event* – whatever that was – I went into a sort of waking coma. I sat in the bed of the funny farm, staring at the wall. Something woke me up. Maybe it was my mum's voice. Maybe I'd decided I'd had enough of this self-indulgent shit. Whatever it was, I decided right then and there I'd never let myself think about it. Instinct, I guess.'

'Fuck, Ells.'

'Yeah.'

'But that's not a hallucination. You didn't see anything. In fact, you did the opposite. What makes you think you imagined Kayden?'

'I guess because it was hazy, that first time... but just now, when he was standing across the street, he was much clearer.'

'If I got my hands on the bastard who pushed you into that pond, Ells...' He gripped the edge of the table. His temples pulsed and he glared at me, his cheeks turning red. 'I'd end them. That's it. I'd end their goddamn lives.'

'But that's the thing. Paisley sounded convincing when she told me he was dead.'

He snorted. 'This is Paisley the manipulator, the woman you think abused Kayden when he was a kid?'

'Yeah. But I don't have any concrete evidence. She was always a little strange toward him, overly possessive. And there was this kiss one time. It lingered for way too long. And when she looked at me afterward, it wasn't like a mother looking at her daughter-in-law. It was like she was competing for his affection.'

'Jesus Christ. That's sick.'

'Yes, it is.'

'We need to go up there.'

'Where?'

He narrowed his eyes. 'Where do you think? Scotland, to their village. We need to go to the grave and see it for ourselves. We need to visit this Paisley woman and tell her she has the stupidest fucking name in the universe. *Paisley*.'

I laughed, stunned he could draw that out of me despite the circumstances. He chuckled and then we fell silent. 'Would you really do that, go up there with me?'

'Of course I would. We need to get to the bottom of this. She said she went to the funeral, right? Well, let's see this grave for ourselves. Let's see if it's real. Let's see this note, if the police have let her keep it. Let's *see*. Because what other choice do you have, sitting around here wondering if you're going crazy? We'll go this weekend.'

I rallied at the thought of taking action instead of waiting for things to happen *to* me. 'But I don't drive. Do you?' I'd never seen him arrive at work in a car. 'Getting there without a car would be a nightmare. Even with a car we'd have to find somewhere to stay. The drive's eight hours, if the traffic's good.'

'I've got a licence, but no, no car. But I can rent one. And we'll rent a nice cottage somewhere. Make a weekend of it.'

'What a holiday,' I commented drily.

He threw his champagne back in one giant mouthful, and then wiped his mouth. 'Don't knock it, Ells. A weekend away with you is a dream come true. And if we have to go skulking around a graveyard, well, that's just a necessary evil.'

It would calm me down somewhat to lay my eyes on the grave. Once I'd seen it, I could attribute my visions of Kayden to stress and sleeplessness. I could burn away this period of my life, leave the ground fresh and fertile for whatever the future might bring. And if it wasn't there, that meant Paisley had lied, and I'd have to find a way to deal with Kayden.

Either way, I'd *know*.

Because right then I felt like I was in a pitch-black room, no idea which direction led to the exit and which direction led to deeper darkness.

'Let's do it. And thank you. For not running away from me. For not calling me a psycho. You didn't expect this baggage.'

He waved a hand. 'It's nothing. Honestly. It's what any decent bloke would do.'

'But that's the thing. There aren't many decent blokes around these days. At least in my experience.'

'Then your experience is a damn shame. Because you don't deserve any of this, Ells. I mean that.'

His words heartened me. It felt so good to finally have an ally.

36

I spent the rest of the week on the lookout for Kayden, going through the motions at work. Blakelyn rang me to tell me she'd managed to get a few more of the reviews removed, but the majority were going to remain on the website. When I asked if they were affecting pre-order sales, she made a vague sound, an audible shrug, and I had my answer.

Kayden didn't show his face. There were no more bricks through my window and, if it wasn't for my desperate need to know if I'd imagined Kayden staring at me from across the street, I might've cancelled the trip and tried to put the craziness behind me.

But I'd be naïve to think this was the end of it. It was only a short reprieve, and if I allowed myself to get too comfortable the abuse would start again.

Freddy stayed at my flat every night leading up to Saturday. We didn't discuss it. It simply happened, as though we'd been planning it all along. It was easy to forget – at least for hours at a time – about all that had happened when I had him to focus on.

On Saturday morning, we packed weekend bags and loaded them into the boot of his rented silver Ford Mondeo, gleaming in the sun. As he stood from the driver's seat, resting his elbows on the roof, it was like we were going on a weekend trip for the sheer pleasure of it: as though Paisley wasn't waiting for us at the end of our journey.

'Shall we play a game?' Freddy drummed his fingers on the wheel as we drove down the motorway. The traffic was light and we were making good time. 'Maybe I spy?'

'I hardly think that would work.' I smiled. 'We're passing everything too quickly.'

'Nah, we'll play it with stuff in the car.'

'Then it'll be too easy.'

'All right, clever clogs. What game shall we play then?'

I thought for a moment. 'What about I say a sentence for a story, and then you say one? I used to play that with Mum when I was a kid...' I swallowed and glanced out the window. I hadn't spoken to Mum since our argument concerning the bills. 'You start. My mind's gone blank.'

It had gone blank every day that week when I tried to sit at my laptop and draw some words out of myself. I would stare at the empty page, willing myself to fill it, even if that meant flooding it with bad words: words I would delete. But I hadn't progressed past a paragraph all week. My mind was consumed, both with my predicament and with Freddy's rock-hard body pushed against mine.

'I'm not much of a writer, Ells.'

'Liar. You wrote those song lyrics.'

He grinned at me, glancing out of the corner of his eye. 'Do you always have an answer for everything?'

'I try to.'

'All right, *fine*. Um... "There once was a woman who forgot how to love."'

'Jeez, Freddy. I thought you said you weren't much of a writer. That's genius.'

'You're mocking me.'

I shook my head. 'I'm not.'

'Fine, then thank you. But please never say *jeez* again.'

I giggled. 'Fair enough... "But then she met a man, with intense eyes and an easy smile."'

'Like this smile, you mean?' He grinned widely.

'I'm not talking about you, if that's what you're trying to imply.'

'Course. Keep telling yourself that.'

'Anyway, it's your turn.'

He tapped his chin in a melodramatic thinking pose, and then nodded. 'We're allowed long sentences, right?'

'I don't see why not.'

He chuckled. 'You might regret that. So... "The woman fell in love with the man's smile straight away, but then she started to get curious about other parts of him, so she lured him to Scotland and they booked a hotel room, and the second they were in the room she pounced on him and started doing the most depraved sexual things she could think of, really bloody dirty stuff, and to be honest he was an innocent lad and didn't know how to react to this, but he went along with it, but this woman, well, she was so sex-crazed, a certified nympho you could say, and she was simply too much to handle, so in the end he had to tell her, I'm sorry, kind lady, but I'm simply too inexperienced to be able to handle the sexual, uh, the sexual fire you're bringing, and I'll be on my way now."'

I was laughing like a loon, my hands on my belly. 'You're such a dick. Honestly. As if you'd react like that anyway.'

'True. But I thought we weren't talking about me.'

'Fuck.'

'That, my sweet Ellie, is what they call a checkmate.'

37

Once, we were in bed together and Kayden was running his fingers through my hair, always running his fingers through my hair, as though he thought he could reach through my scalp and into my brain and access my thoughts. In fact, this was precisely what I thought he was doing: the same way I had divined the truth about his abuse.

I liked the feeling of his fingertips in my mind, swirling through my memories and my hopes and my dreams. I imagined we were fusing together in this way. We were melting into each other, and one day we would be able to communicate without the need of speech.

'I love you, Lottie,' he said to me. 'I've never known what it's like to love or be loved. With my Mum... with how she is. And with my dad away so much... Girls my age are so silly. But you, I love you so much. I love you more than life itself. When we go away together, when we start our new life, I want to do it as husband and wife.'

'I love you too,' I told him, though I didn't feel it. I didn't feel much of anything in those days. I was numb, woefully distanced from myself, chemically muted. Other-dazed. 'And I'll never stop loving you. I want to be your wife. I want us to have children together. But...'

And here comes the great contradiction in my mind back then.

I was proud of my ability to reach into the magical realms, as I deemed it, proud of the voices which spoke to me in the wind and the trees, even if they were malicious at times. But I was also terrified of my children inheriting this ability, because perhaps I knew deep down – where it counts – how awful this truly was. Perhaps there was some part of me separate from myself, an unbiased onlooker, that knew there was a problem, a serious problem that needed to be fixed.

I explained this to Kayden, and I began to cry. I cried the same way Kayden often did after I rode him, after I straddled him and pumped my hips violently up and down, my fingernails buried in his chest, and he gawped up at me with confusion and lust and resentment and hate and love buried within the blueness of his eyes.

He said, 'You can't say that. You're incredible. What you have, your ability to see things others could only dream of, I'd give anything to be able to do that. To escape reality, to truly escape it, to not have to live in this mundane hell the rest of us inhabit.'

Kayden was such a good speaker, even at that young age, always able to sound like he'd studied a topic for years.

I sat up, nodding, drinking in the poison of his words. 'Do you really think so?'

He cradled my face in his hands. We were so romantic, obsessed with each other, when it came to anything but the sexual. I always led the way in that regard, but with everything else we were equals, we were together. 'You're magic, Lottie. You're the most special, most magic, most brilliant person I've ever met in my whole life. I love you and I don't think you should be ashamed of your gifts.'

~

I have paused, because I am nearing the end and I don't particularly want to tell it. I need to state something, however, before I finish this tragic tale.

Everything I have written thus far has been a reflection of how I experienced things at the time, as best as I can remember them. There are thousands of small moments I am leaving out, but the bulk of it – meeting Kayden, loving Kayden – is how I experienced those days, but sequential experience is one of the trickiest things for a schizophrenic... no, no, that's not fair. I can't say *for a schizophrenic* as though we're one entity, a single thing that can be described.

The truth is most people who have been afflicted with this disease would not do what I did. They would not have allowed themselves to luxuriously wallow in their delusions. They wouldn't have *welcomed* it.

But I did. I wished for the voices – the make-believe voices and Kayden's reassuring words – to be true, and so they were true. You might read that and think to yourself, *But she said she was so terrified of her illness she didn't want to have children, in case they inherited it.*

This is true, and it is also true I was in love with my illness and thought it made me special. I can only state how I felt, because trying to make sense of it is impossible.

I was, being frank, a madwoman. And the Other enjoyed my madness. The Other relished in it. I am sorry, if there is a reader of these words... I am sorry for being obtuse, but I refuse to extricate this in words before I extricated it within myself.

I think I should write about the one major argument Kayden and I had before I reveal the truth of the matter. Or at least some of the truth. Because this argument was real. It was the realest thing we'd ever discussed. It lasted hours and it got physical and

I can't understand why he was adamant about this, especially after what came after: especially after all I learned.

It didn't make any sense, but I suppose it is often the way with abusers and their victims.

As with my illness, they hate them – of course they hate them, they rightfully hate them – but they love them too. They love them in a corrupted and impure way, a brand of emotion that should never exist, but it's there, nestled deeply and twisting its way through the person until they can't remember what it's like to be unscarred.

38

After a nine-hour drive, we arrived at our accommodation at the edge of the village. The sun was a stubborn white orb in the sky, casting its rays over the loping hillsides that surrounded the picturesque cottage where we'd rented a room.

'What do you think?' Freddy said, as we sat in the car park outside this fairy-tale place. 'Shall we go and see her tonight, go to the graveyard, or get some dinner and sort all that tomorrow?'

'Let's handle it tomorrow. We'll get up early and see her, swing by the cemetery, and then drive back. I need to be back tomorrow evening for work on Monday.'

'Sounds like a plan.'

We left the car and checked in, and then went to our room. It was a lovely, cosy slice of the cottage, with rustic rafters and a window made of wrought black iron, the glass clouded so it distorted the sunlight as it shafted downward. I stood at the window, looking out upon the garden, wilder and less meticulous than Mum's. Vines and ivy and flowers of every colour proliferated. It was quite beautiful.

Freddy walked up behind me, wrapping his arms around my

waist and pressing his body against my back. 'How does it feel, being back here?'

'Not as bad as I thought it would be. But I think that's because you're here.'

I turned and kissed him, hard, passionately, kissed him like I'd never been hurt before and would never be hurt again.

The following morning, I stared across the street at Paisley's house, a building comprised of cobblestones that appeared to have been hastily thrown together. Creepers covered it from bottom to top, and the lane leading to the front door was a jungle. I imagined Mum cringing if she'd ever had cause to set eyes upon it.

It looked like a forgotten place, a dying place.

'Are you sure you want to do this?' Freddy took my hand in his. 'Say the word and we'll turn back right now. Maybe this was a mistake.'

'Do I look that bad?' I could hear in my voice it was a silly question.

There was a quiver that threw me back years, to the times I'd visited with Kayden, when he'd roughly dug his fingers into my arm until the skin bruised. 'Don't say a fucking word, cunt.' That's what he'd said: my husband, the man I'd given myself to. And what did I do? I took it. I nodded meekly, a veritable mouse. I let it happen.

'Ells.' Freddy smoothed the hair behind my ear, tickling me.

'Yeah?'

'I said it's your choice.'

'Sorry. I was miles away.'

He waited, giving me the space to think. I was grateful for it. I knew it would be easier to tell if Paisley was lying if I confronted her in person.

And there was something else. I was done living in fear of the Hunter clan. I was done making decisions based on the terror that had captured me for so many years, which *still* captured me.

I grabbed the door handle before I could scare myself out of it. 'Let's get this over with.'

I bolted from the car and strode down the path, stepping between the overgrown weeds, and hammered my fist against the door. Paisley coughed from deeper in the house, a violent smoker's expulsion. The coughing got closer and closer. Then the door opened.

Paisley was a large woman, made larger by the giant T-shirts she wore. That morning it was white with blotches of yellow something here and there. Her hair hung grey and listless on her shoulders, and a cigarette was jammed between her teeth. Her eyes were Kayden's bright blues, lighting up when she saw me, as she sucked on her cigarette and brought it from her mouth to speak. 'Well, look here. Her Highness finally graces me with her presence.'

'Hello, Paisley.' It was better to keep this civil, if possible. 'Would it be okay if we came in and talked? This is Freddy, by the way, my...'

I wasn't sure how to describe him, but then he darted forward and offered his hand. 'I'm her boyfriend. Freddy Jenkins.'

She stared at his hand, and then turned and paced into her house. 'Come on. I'll make us some tea.'

'I'm not thirsty–'

'Don't be rude,' she called over her shoulder, marching into the kitchen at the end of the hall.

Freddy and I glanced at each other. 'Why did you say you're my boyfriend?'

'Do you have a problem with it?'

I thought for a moment. 'No, I don't think so.'

'Good.' He grinned, waving a hand. 'Then after you, *girlfriend.*'

We walked into the house, which reeked of cigarette smoke and a general staleness, as though she hadn't hoovered in weeks, months, years.

The walls of the hallway were covered in photos of Kayden, countless eyes staring at me as we made our way toward the entrance to the living room. Many of them were of Kayden as a child – bright-eyed, optimistic – and then as a sulky teenager, and finally as a sociopathic man, black-haired and then grey-haired, with his signature love-me smirk in each one.

'Think she's got enough photos?' Freddy whispered as we walked into the living room.

'Tell me about it.'

The living room was absurdly messy, with clothes piled up in seemingly random places. There were newspapers and magazines and more photographs of Kayden, dozens if not hundreds of them lining every section of the wall.

Freddy gazed around, his mouth falling open. 'Fuck me.'

I nodded to a patch of her musty-looking sofa that was free from her hoarder's detritus. 'Let's sit down. She'll insist we drink some of her tea. She always does. I guess she thinks it makes her a good hostess.'

'Hard to be a good hostess in this shithole.'

'Hush, Freddy. She might hear.'

'Look at this fucking freak show.' He sighed as we sat. 'There's loving your kid and then there's this. This is weird.'

'Fine. But we're not here to give her a psychological evaluation.'

'Thank God for that.'

Paisley returned with a tray holding three mugs of tea and a plate of shortcake biscuits. The coffee table was heavy with newspapers and magazines and dirty dishes, so she placed the tray at the very edge, pushing until the papers slid aside enough to give her room. I cringed when a plate clattered to the floor, but she didn't flinch. I supposed she was used to it.

Sorry about the mess, any regular person would say, but Paisley wasn't capable of being sorry about anything.

'So.' She lit a cigarette with a silver flip lighter and inhaled half of it in one drag. The room stank. 'What brings you to these parts?'

'I'm here to visit Kayden's grave. I thought it would be respectful if I checked in with you first.'

I waited for her to flinch, for panic to take possession of her features. I purposefully hadn't warned her of my visit. I didn't want to give her time to prepare a fake gravesite, for her to buy a headstone and place it in the cemetery. It was the sort of deranged thing I could imagine her doing.

'I think that's quite right.' She seemed completely at ease as she flicked cigarette ash into a coffee mug which sat on the arm of the chair. 'Please, have some tea.'

'I'm not thirsty,' Freddy said, as I reached for the mug.

I shot him a look. I'd already told him she wouldn't talk to us if we didn't indulge her. It had been the same when I visited with Kayden. She told herself countless lies so she didn't hate herself, and being a good hostess was just one more. Freddy sighed and picked up his mug, and we both sipped.

It was bitter and sour and not at all appealing. I smiled and made *hmm* noises. 'Thank you, Paisley. That's lovely. We're going to go to his grave in a bit, but I also wanted to discuss...'

I wasn't sure how to phrase this tactfully.

'The reviews,' Freddy went on. 'For her books. And at her workplace. We're going to need you to remove them.'

She blew smoke. 'I'm sorry, lad, but I find it very strange that you're speaking for my daughter-in-law.'

Don't call me your fucking daughter-in-law, you crazy bitch, I almost screamed, but I kept myself under control. 'Paisley, I understand you're upset. Kayden and I didn't exactly have the best marriage. And I'm sorry about his suicide. But torturing me isn't going to change that.'

'Who said I'm behind them anyway?'

I stared at her, trying to read her expression, but it was difficult when she kept half her face shielded with her hand as she smoked. '*Are* you behind them?'

'Look around here. Do you see a computer?' The smoke was shimmering strangely around her face, as though there was far too much of it.

'Don't play games with us.' Freddy leaned forward, his voice strained. Did he see the smoke too? 'She asked you a direct question. She deserves a direct answer.'

'Calm yourself, boy. This has nothing to do with you. Drink your tea and wait until you're spoken to.'

I placed my hand on Freddy's arm as he tensed up, getting ready to shout at her. He gritted his teeth and sat back, raising his hands as if to say, *Fine, you handle her then*. He was on edge, the same way I felt. My throat was dry and everything seemed too sharp, too close somehow.

We sat in silence for a time, the three of us sipping from our mugs, and then I murmured, 'I think I deserve the truth. After everything your son put me through.'

'Please, Ellie, I refuse to listen to your poison.'

'Fine, forget that.' It was becoming more difficult to speak. Much better to throw my bitter disgusting tea in her bitter disgusting face. At least the smoke had stopped shifting and expanding, but my head pulsed, my skin itched. 'But I deserve to know, at the very least, if you plan on keeping this up. Hiring people to ring me at work. Hiring people to fucking *attack* me in parks. Hiring people to sabotage my career: my dream career and my regular job. It's wrong. I don't think I deserve it.'

A liquid smile spread across her face. Her eyes glimmered with the same wetness; for a moment the glimmering seemed to dance, the same way the smoke had. I blinked and willed it to return to normal. 'You silly girl. This isn't about what *you* deserve.'

'What's that supposed to mean?'

'You'll see. Sooner or later, it will become clear.'

'So you're admitting you're behind it?' My voice rose and Freddy made to touch my shoulder, but I moved away from him. 'I'm sick of your snide hints. Tell me the fucking *truth*.'

'I won't be spoken to like this in my own home. Either keep your tone civil or get out. Your choice.'

I bit down another wave of vitriol, knocking back the rest of my tea and slamming the mug onto the tray. 'Hmm, delicious.'

'Oh, Ellie, I do feel sorry for you.'

'I'm dying to know why, Paisley.'

'Because you truly have no idea what's going on here, not in the slightest. You think you could cause my son's suicide and go on with your life as if nothing had happened. You think you can come up here and disrespect me in my own home and there won't be any consequences. But there will be. And when it happens, when you learn the truth, it's going to break you. It's going to shatter you into a million pieces. And I'll be laughing. You took my baby from me. My Kayden. You need to pay.'

I bolted to my feet, picking up the mug and throwing it at the wall.

It smashed loudly, shattered, pieces flying everywhere.

I waved my hand in her face as she sat, unperturbed, taking a casual drag of her cigarette. My feet were unsteady beneath me. Simply standing was difficult. 'You're going to have those reviews removed. If you don't, I won't go to the police. If you don't have those reviews taken down *immediately*, Paisley, I'm going to kill you. Do you understand, you disgusting woman, you deranged paedo cunt? I'm going to sneak in here one night and stab you until my arm is so tired I can't move it anymore. I swear to God.'

'Whatever you say, Ellie. Whatever you say.'

'Come on.' Freddy's hands were on my shoulders. 'She's not worth it.'

He led me out of the house.

I was trembling, ready to march in there and bury my fingernails in her eyes, which had reminded me too violently of my husband. I marched toward the car. 'The cemetery. I have to see it.'

'Oh, and Ellie?' I turned to find Paisley standing at the door, a sick grin on her face. 'I *really* hope you enjoyed the tea.'

I ignored her and climbed into the car, squeezing my knees hard, fingernails stabbing into skin. 'What the hell did she mean by that?'

'No idea.' Freddy started the engine.

I looked up at the country road as he guided us down it, and then the road was splitting right down the middle, like paper, and thousands of insects were crawling out from the cracked concrete and skittering over the surrounding hills. The hills were teeming and black with them.

The faces of the insects magnified, expanding across my vision, and they were Kayden. Every single one of them was Kayden: he was laughing and frowning and baring his teeth, and blood was dripping electric-red over his gums, pulsing with light. I'd never seen a red so stark and bright and ugly. Another face opened its mouth in a twisted giant scream.

I clamped my hands over my ears, blocking it out.

And then it hit me. I remembered the weird shifting of the smoke and the glimmering in her eyes. The pulsing in my head became more intense. 'That bitch. That lunatic.'

'Are you seeing this?' Freddy's voice was jagged. 'Ells, what's happening?'

'She drugged the tea. She drugged the fucking tea.'

Freddy roared and jerked the wheel to the side, the car snapping sideways.

We veered off the road and skidded onto the grass, and then we were spinning around and around and around.

39

'Ells, calm down. Open your eyes.'

I was screaming. It was a reasonable thing for me to do, because the car was spinning and we were about to crash and die. But then I realised we weren't spinning at all. The car had come to a stop at the side of the road and the motion had ceased, or it had never existed at all.

I opened my eyes, risking a look at the fields.

The creatures had gone, but the sunlight was doing bizarre things, whispering across the sky like a giant invisible hand was cutting a knife across the heavens, the harsh metal catching the glinting yellow. I looked closely and saw it was spelling words.

Mother. Death. Sorry. Kayden.

I blinked and rubbed my eyes. The words vanished.

Everything seemed too close. The sun was going to fall into the car. A fly buzzed past, and for a moment it was inside the car. Then it buzzed away, sinking through the window, and it was gone. Its wings made taunting noises, words dim beneath the hissing. 'You pushed and pushed and pushed...'

Freddy glanced at the road. 'Clowns. I hate clowns.'

'It was insects. No, him. It was him. *They* were him.'

'Ells, I doubt we're seeing the same thing. I mean, that'd be pretty damn unlikely.'

I laughed, though it wasn't funny. I kept laughing, and the laughter grew in my belly until I was sure it was going to burst out of my skin and rupture me. The jagged feeling tore through my middle and suddenly the car was a room which reeked of bleach and sweat. And there were faces staring at me from the car's front window, and red hair, fire-red hair, flickering as a mouth shaped an uncertain smile.

'What the hell is this stuff?'

'No idea. Not shrooms. At least not any sort I've ever done. Maybe acid.'

'What do we do?'

'There's nothing we can do. Except ride it out.'

I shivered, wrapping my arms around myself. 'I don't like this. I thought we crashed. I thought we were spinning.'

He pulled me into a hug, stroking my hair. He kissed my cheek and whispered in my ear, 'I pulled onto the side of the road and parked, that's all. The car's fine. We're fine. I think we'll leave the car here, go back to the room, sleep this off and pick it up later. We might have to get another night at the hotel. And you'll have to pull a sickie tomorrow. See? Sorted. No need to panic.'

'No need to panic,' I repeated dully, as I felt doors trying to open in my mind.

Kayden reared up in my imagination, his lips pressed into a knife-sharp grimace, his eyes blazing, like the hair from the room with the bleach. Like the sharpness of the knife in the sunlight. Everything melted together. Kayden captured it and his eyes became aborted children, two pink grotesques with umbilical cords wrapped around their necks. 'Did you really think you could escape me, you wee slut? Do what you were made to do and get on your fucking knees.'

I tried to suck in air but there wasn't enough. I was sure somebody, somehow, had siphoned the oxygen out of the atmosphere and I was going to choke.

I turned and clawed at the door handle, fumbled, pulled it open and stumbled out onto the country road.

'Where are you going?' Freddy trailed after me.

'I can't. Stay here. I have to. Walk.'

'Yeah, me too. But which way was it? I can't remember.'

I looked up and down the road. Paisley's house was still within view. I thought about going back there and mutilating her for what she'd done, but the overgrown plants in her garden were shivering and beckoning.

Something was crawling through the foliage. It would leap out at us the moment we came too close. A baby, on all fours, an abandoned baby disturbing the leaves and making them dance.

'I think if we go this way...' I pointed in the direction opposite her house. 'We should be okay, because that's the way we drove in, right?'

Freddy nodded seriously. 'I think so. Yes. That makes sense.'

He took my hand and I squeezed it too tightly, desperate for the contact. 'Maybe we should go back and hurt her. Paisley. Maybe we should kill her for this. It's fucked.'

He laughed darkly. 'Yeah, but then we'd end up in prison, Ells. And I've got no desire for that. Well, unless it meant protecting you. I think I'd go to prison for you.'

'Don't say stupid things.'

It wasn't his fault his hair was not red. It wasn't his fault he didn't smell lifelessly clean and clinical and that his smile wasn't unsure and that he'd never cradled me as rain hammered above. It wasn't his fault the foetuses from Kayden's eyes were crawling toward me from the fields, choking and gasping as their umbilicals tightened around their innocent throats.

It wasn't his fault a door was opening inside of me, a door I needed to keep closed, locked tight.

But I hated Freddy right then, truly hated him, for saying such a ridiculous thing.

He was not Theo. He hadn't loved me. He hadn't left me. He hadn't sat at my side as I'd–

'No, no, no.'

Couldn't look there, couldn't *ever* look there.

'Ells, it's okay.'

Freddy moved to touch me but I slapped his hand away, walking down the path.

Because it wasn't okay. Nothing would ever be okay again.

40

It took us half the day to walk back to the village. We kept stopping to gaze in awe at the surrounding countryside, at the grass which waved like thousands of tiny people were buried down there, stirring it. Whatever drug Paisley had spiked us with made me forget how the staring would end each time: made me forget that the unseen creatures would invariably turn into little Kaydens, millions of them swarming toward me. And then I would turn away, head bowed, focusing on my footsteps, only my footsteps, because everything else was too painful.

I felt my mind turning inward and I rebelled against it.

Normally I was able to force my attention away from the locked doors inside myself: from the year I'd lost as a child.

But each time I turned into myself, I felt how weak I was, how tempted I was to kick the doors down and see what the hell had happened. It seemed harmless with the aid of the hallucinogenic. The idea that something which had happened so long ago could cause me pain seemed laughable.

I laughed.

I collapsed at the edge of the path and gripped my side and

blazed my laughter into the sky. Freddy fell beside me and we both became feral in our mirth, not caring when people passed us by, giving us strange looks. But then the laughter broke into a sob and I was weeping, weeping without knowing why. No, that wasn't right. I'd always known, always felt it, and maybe that was why Kayden had found me such pliable prey.

Maybe it was the guilt of what I'd done, what I'd lost, which caused me to lie beneath him silently, as he fucked me, as he raped me, *raped* me. As he collapsed atop me and drove inside of me and I lay there, brain-dead, because the woman I could've been *could* never be. There was no going back, so fuck it, let him use my body in whichever way satisfied his sick hunger. Let him punch and kick and bite and humiliate me.

I'd never thought of it in these terms before. But then I'd never *let* myself come into contact with this particular piece of misery. With the crying, the squealing, and the legs kicking, and I was falling and falling and then Freddy had his hand wrapped around mine.

'Ellie, you have to stop crying. You need to calm down.'

'Calm. Down. Calm fucking *down*?'

He pulled me to my feet when somebody approached us. 'Seriously. Somebody might get angry. Somebody might try to hurt us.'

I glanced over my shoulder. It was an elderly man with his hands stretched out, speaking but silently, opening and closing his mouth like he was trying to freak us out. His hair was grey, Kayden-grey, and Freddy was right. He was dangerous. He held two bones, the ends carved into sharp points. He'd killed somebody and ripped out pieces of them, as Kayden had torn out pieces of me; as Theo had ripped out pieces of me. As *I* had ripped out pieces of me by letting it happen.

We fled, walking until we came to the outskirts of the village, and then Freddy tugged on my hand. He pointed off to the left. I'd been staring at the ground counting the stones, for some reason, thinking it was very important. Perhaps because counting was easier than focusing on the tiny death-blue fingertips attempting to claw up between them, the fingernails splintered and weeping with blood.

It was the cemetery, its doors thrown open as though in invitation.

'What?'

'Kayden, remember? We might as well check.'

I nodded vigorously, as though I could push past the fear of what we might find. Or not find. 'Let's go. Maybe I'll piss on his grave if it's quiet.'

Freddy tilted his head at me, a soft frown touching his lips.

I didn't like the way he was looking at me. It was too intimate, and I wondered what Theo would think, my dear sweet Theo, if he knew a man was looking at me with so much concern. But no, no – I had to remind myself, keep reminding myself that Theo was a boy from a long time ago. He had nothing to do with me.

The past and the present were collapsing together, time shortening, as though the clean room and the regret and the soft eyes had happened only yesterday.

'Holy shit. Look. Are you seeing this too?'

Without realising, I'd been walking next to Freddy, my legs moving without my say-so. I forced myself to look up, ignoring the thousand spectres of the past which haunted endlessly at the periphery.

Freddy had stopped in front of a brand-new marble headstone. I walked up beside him and stared at the words.

Kayden Hunter
Beloved Son
1970 – 2021

'Read it.' I had to force my words past the tears. I remembered Kayden in the glass. I remembered him in the street. I remembered his eyes behind the hockey mask. 'Freddy. I have to hear you read it.'

'Kayden Hunter. Beloved son…'

I fell to my knees and buried my fingers in the earth. The headstone was shivering with my tears, the words distorting, but they refused to change. There it was: evidence of his death. Which meant I was as mad as Mother, like Paisley had branded me.

'No.' I clawed at the mud, scraped it under my fingernails. 'We have to dig. Freddy. We have to dig. This isn't Kayden. I *saw* him. I saw him, not just in the glass. In the daylight. He was real. I wasn't on acid then.'

I began to paw at the dirt. Freddy fell to his knees beside me and joined in. If he'd been sober perhaps he would've realised how insane this was, but neither of us cared. We were in this together.

We clawed and clawed and got nowhere.

Somebody yelled at us, their voice deep and booming. It was a doctor, a man in a long white coat, too clean for the surroundings. 'Get away, will you! What's the bloody matter with you!'

Freddy hauled me to my feet, but I refused to move. I continued to stare at the headstone, my eyes fixed on the fact of Kayden's death. The only other option was that Paisley had somehow learned we were visiting in advance and she'd falsified the grave, but how would she know?

'Fuck's sake, Ells.' Freddy scooped me into his arms, tipping my whole world sideways, and wrestled me to his chest as he made for the exit. 'I'm taking you back to the room. We need to sleep this shit off.'

41

I was sitting on the toilet and staring at the floor, at the tiles which were shimmering and converging and then flying apart in fascinating interplays. I wasn't sure how much time had passed since I'd sat down. It could've been a few minutes or a few hours.

Freddy snored loudly from the next room, and the sunlight was a deeper shade, a blood-red shade, and I thought it looked quite compelling as it glowed against the clouded glass.

I stood on shaky legs, wandering over to the sink and running the water. I splashed cold water in my face, quickly looking away when the water turned dirty and brown as it swirled down the plughole.

I gazed at myself in the mirror, but then my reflection shimmered and the mirror became a window.

A little girl with her hair messily brushed and a nervous look on her face. It was a few years after Dad died and things were not good at home. A young boy skipped over, his hair a tangled and messy red, constellations of freckles across his cheeks and a brave nervous smile on his face.

'Hello. I'm Theo.'

The girl toed the ground. With a jolt of shock I realised something. The girl was me.

'I'm Ellie.' The girl bit her lip, debating, and then reached into her pocket and took out a daisy bracelet she'd wrapped in a piece of tissue paper. 'Do you want this? I made it and I wanted to give it to somebody, but there's nobody to give it to. But you can have it.'

The boy's grin widened. 'Yeah. Cool. I like your voice.'

She giggled. 'Why?'

'It's posh. It's cool. Thank you.'

He took the daisy chain and tucked it into his schoolbag as though it was the most precious thing he'd ever encountered.

The mirror shimmered and they were older, this boy and girl, crouched inside a bus stop as rain slashed against the plastic covering and became hammers above them. The girl laughed and handed the boy a glass bottle. 'You're such a lightweight.' She prodded him when he groaned and waved it away. 'Come on, Theo. One more sip.'

'You're a bully.' The boy laughed and took it from her. 'If I didn't love you, I'd hate you.'

'Wow, that's like poetry. You're talented.'

'You're taking the piss.'

'A little, yeah. But I mean it. You're the most talented person I know.'

The boy and the girl converged on each other. I wondered if I should look away in shame as they ravaged each other, not caring they were in public, not caring somebody could pop their head into the bus stop any moment.

I felt Theo's breath on my neck. I felt him inside of me and I cringed, because I never thought about Theo in a sexual way. I never allowed myself. He'd been a boy when we were together.

'I love you.' His lips smeared the girl's cheek as he finished. 'I love you so fucking much.'

'I love you too,' the girl gasped, clawing at his face. 'Promise you'll never leave me. No matter what happens. Promise.'

'I promise. It's me and you, forever. Look.'

The boy leaned down and reached into his bag. He brought out a plastic wrapping. The girl giggled because she thought it was weed. She was excited. But she was more excited when she saw what it truly was: the daisy chain, crumbled with time, its outline imprinted upon some tissue paper.

I gripped the edge of the sink and let out a jagged cry, tears streaming down my cheeks, as the mirror-window shifted and I saw the girl sitting in Theo's bedroom. She had her legs folded on a rickety wooden chair, sun dappling her face, as he moved his paintbrush over the canvas and smiled at her occasionally.

'Stop moving,' he said.

'I'm not moving.'

'You're talking. That means you're moving.'

'I'm only talking because you spoke to me first.'

He laughed. 'You're too smart for me.'

She sat as still as she could as the sun tracked the day across her face, and finally he was finished and she skipped over to the canvas. She gasped and covered her mouth with her hand.

And, standing in the bathroom in the cottage, I did the same. I clamped my hand over my mouth to trap the emotion: emotion I'd never faced, never *considered* facing.

'You've made me beautiful.'

Theo turned to her, reaching up with paint-flecked fingertips and stroking her cheek. 'You *are* beautiful.'

They fell upon each other, fuelled by the knowledge this was the right thing, the only thing that mattered in the whole world. They didn't need anything else. They collapsed against each other and they tore each other to pieces, and then the mirror shifted and I was staring at Theo and the girl in a park.

183

The girl was staring down at something, a small white object.

A pregnancy test, the girl was staring down at a pregnancy test.

'Maybe it's not right,' Theo said.

'It's the fifth one.'

'Fuck. Fuck. *Fuck.*'

'Yeah.'

I could barely stand, but I was afraid if I moved away from the window the film would stop. I'd spent my whole life running from this, but I couldn't ignore it now, not when it was laid out so clearly for me.

I saw the girl waddling through the hallways of the school, her cheeks blooming when the other kids sniggered and tossed names at her.

Slut. Whale. Tart.

I saw a younger Georgia throwing herself at a group of lads, waving her fingers in their faces and calling them every wicked name she could think of.

And then the girl was in a hospital bed and she was staring down at her child, at the boy she would never give a name to, because she'd agreed – and Theo had agreed – it was best to give him up for adoption. Theo was sitting beside the bed with his mother and his father stood behind him, his father's hand firmly planted upon his shoulder, as though ready to drag him back if he tried to hold his baby.

'It's for the best,' Theo's father said, his voice iron and unflinching. 'Come on. Say goodbye.'

But how could a person say goodbye when they had never properly said hello?

I dropped onto the bathroom floor and buried my face in my hands, wracked by savage sobs. I didn't need the mirror anymore.

The doors in my mind flew open and the memories spilled into me, fuelled by the acid or whatever it was.

I felt the heat of my child in my arms. I felt the wetness of his lips as I leaned down and laid a kiss against him. I felt his hand coiling around two of my fingers, and then Mum was there, taking him from me. She frowned over the top of his head and I could see she knew it was a mistake.

But there had been *talks*, endless fucking talks.

Theo's parents had pushed for putting the boy up for adoption as though their lives depended on it, and Mum was in no state to defend me. I'd felt like I was being pulled apart, one hand clinging to the notion of young motherhood and the other gripped tightly around my future.

But in the end I was simply a fourteen-year-old girl, a naïve and foolish child, who thought I could give away the most important thing in my life without any consequences.

But there were consequences.

I closed my eyes against the stinging tears and saw myself pacing up and down my bedroom, screaming, tearing fingernails across my midriff as though I was trying to get to my womb: to gouge away the organ that had allowed this to happen.

There I was: straight razor in my hand, the cool metal poised over my vein, when the bathroom door crashed open and Mum charged in. Her eyes cleared for the first time in years when she saw her daughter ready to open herself up.

She dragged me to hospital, and shortly after I was admitted to the psychiatric ward.

And then...

I had sat in a state of paralysis in my room in the mental hospital, arms wrapped around myself, staring at the wall.

I would eat and use the bathroom and take my medication, but then I'd return to my place, gazing, refusing to speak. When Mum visited and told me Theo's parents had moved away because it was *too complicated* to stay – that's how they'd phrased it, apparently, as though our love and our shared connection was meaningless – I said nothing.

My craziness had jolted Mum out of hers. For the first time in my life, she was there for me.

One day, I awoke from this waking sleep with no memory of the pregnancy, with no memory of why Theo had left. I didn't ask, and they didn't tell me. Perhaps they thought they were doing me a favour, but I hated them for it.

My son was out there.

He'd be nineteen years old, in the world someplace with his adopted family, hopefully doing something good, productive.

Freddy strode into the bathroom, finding me in a sob-wrecked ball on the floor.

'Jesus, Ells. What is it? What's wrong?'

I gazed up at him, mumbling something about the past, about Theo, about family, but it came out gnarled in animal agony.

He sat on the bathroom floor and pulled me into his lap, stroking my hair over and over, whispering he was here for me, he'd make it all better. But I'd given up my right to feel at peace the moment I'd given away my child.

Where was he? Who was he? Was he a good person? Was he kind to his adopted parents? Did he have a girlfriend, a passion? Was he in university?

If I ran into him on the street, I'd be a stranger, just another passing face.

'Ells, what's wrong?'

'I can't say.' I pressed my face into his shirt and wept. 'Hold me. Please, Freddy.'

He hugged me tighter.

42

I woke with tension in my back, peeling my eyes open and staring at the bathroom ceiling. We'd fallen asleep on the floor, Freddy sprawled against the wall, his chin coming to rest against his chest as he drew in loud shivering breaths. I smiled at his snoring for a moment, staring at the way his smirk twitched in his sleep, revelling in how handsome he was.

And then I remembered: the tea, the hallucinogenic, the *past*.

I stood and stumbled over to the sink. My mouth was bone dry and I lapped water greedily, splashing big handfuls in my face over and over.

I stared into the mirror, into my wide panicked eyes. I peered closer and tried to make the glass shift again, the way it had last night, or had that been a dream?

It was difficult to disentangle the events of the previous night when my head felt so cloudy, my thoughts spiralling here and there, impossible to catch. I closed my eyes and willed myself to relive it all: meeting with Paisley, the car crash – no, the car hadn't crashed. I'd imagined that.

The walk. We'd walked to the gravesite and Kayden's stone had proclaimed his death, and then we'd returned and I'd seen it all, as though my memory was playing a film for me.

I saw Theo and our child, our fucking *child*.

I walked over to the toilet and sat on the closed lid, wrapping my hands around my knees and trying to convince myself it had been nothing more than a mad hallucination.

Perhaps I could've believed that if it didn't feel true, as though I'd always known this. It had always been waiting, but I'd simply refused to look there.

Theo's parents convinced him to convince *me* to give the child up, because it was the best thing for our futures. I remembered that now: Theo's serious face, his apologetic eyes, as he nodded and repeated words his father had hurled at him. 'We can't sacrifice our lives for one mistake. We can't give away our futures.'

Well, this was my future, a madwoman who'd blotted out the most important thing in my life and who'd dreamed up my ex-husband. I could forgive myself for the face in the glass, but seeing him standing across the street, grinning at me, as real as any alive person... it meant my mind was more cracked than I'd ever realised.

It also left me with the question of the hockey-mask man.

If it wasn't Kayden, then who?

I let out a whimper as my gaze turned, taking in the sight of Freddy. I thought about how strange he'd acted when his phone rang, and how he always got special treatment at work, got away with things nobody else ever could. But I failed to see how these suspicions were connected to my assault and the rest of it.

No, no, I was letting paranoia get the better of me.

If Paisley was behind the reviews, which she'd basically admitted the previous day with her snide remarks, she was behind the assault too. She was behind all of it.

She'd drugged us, for fuck's sake.

Freddy looked so young in his sleep, so content. He was only six years older than my child, six small years. The thought sickened me and made me question our age gap again.

I needed to speak to Mum, to confirm my hallucinations hadn't lied to me.

I forced myself to stand and pace across the room, nudging Freddy with my foot. 'Wake up, Freddy. We have to go.'

He started, as though emerging from water. 'Shit. What time is it?'

'I'll check my phone.'

I went into the bedroom. The room was surprisingly neat. I'd imagined walking into a war zone, the walls covered in psychotic scrawls, but the bed was made and both our phones were charging on the bedside table. I picked up mine and glanced at the screen.

It was ten. I had several missed calls from work.

'Did we pay for another night?' I turned to Freddy, who stood in the bathroom doorway with his hand on the back of his neck, rubbing softly.

'Yeah. I did it when you were in the bathroom. You were in there for ages, Ells.'

'It was...'

I could barely stand to face it myself. Tears tried to pour from my eyes every time I thought about the bundle, the way he'd stared up at me, confident I'd take care of him. I'd never let anything happen to him. But I had.

I'd given him away like he meant nothing.

Freddy strode across the room and put his hands on my shoulders. 'Are you okay? You're going to feel weird for the rest of the day, maybe the next couple of days, but try not to worry about it. It'll pass.'

'So you're an expert now?' I snapped. It wasn't fair. It wasn't his fault I'd forfeited my chance to be a mother, twice: first by giving away my son and then by aborting Kayden's child.

He let his hands drop. 'I'm trying to help.'

I moved close to him, grabbing onto his chest. 'I'm sorry. Can we just get out of here?'

'It's either that or visit that crazy bitch again and make her pay for what she did to us. I can't believe she did that.'

'I can. She's insane.'

Freddy looked around for a moment and then walked over to his shoes, picking them up and dropping onto the bed. 'I'll run down and get the car, we'll check out, and then we'll put this mad shit behind us. At least we got what we came for though. She admitted it, didn't she? Without coming right out and saying it.'

'Yeah.'

When it happens, when you learn the truth, it's going to break you. It's going to shatter you into a million fucking pieces.

Was she talking about Theo and our child?

But there was no way she could know about that, and certainly no way she could be sure the psychedelics would cause the memory to resurface. She must've been referencing something else. Or she was trying to scare me?

She hadn't denied being behind the reviews. And we'd seen Kayden's grave. In a way Freddy was right. We'd got what we came for.

'Freddy, when you grab the car, can you swing by the cemetery and...'

'Of course.' He didn't need me to go on. He knew I needed to be sure we hadn't dreamed up the headstone bearing my dead husband's name. 'I won't be long.'

'I need to ring work and tell them I won't be in today.'

Freddy smirked. 'That should be fun.'

I rolled my eyes, a smile tugging at the corner of my lips. Freddy was magic if he could make me smile at a time like this.

He left and I sat on the bed, ringing Furniture Care Association.

43

Nigel roared at me when I lied and said I had a stomach bug and I'd overslept, but it was difficult to care when I had my child's cherubic face branded into my mind. It was difficult to summon any emotion when Freddy confirmed Kayden's headstone was still there that morning.

As Freddy drove us down the country road that would lead to the motorway, I felt an all-encompassing numbness move over me, as though nothing mattered and never would again.

My child, my baby, I'd given him away.

What was wrong with me?

Why had I let Theo and his family convince me?

'When we get back, can you take me to my mum's house? I need to speak with her.'

'Of course, Ells. Whatever you need.'

'Thank you.'

Despite knowing in my gut the hallucinations had told the truth, I needed to hear somebody else say it. We'd argued the last time we saw each other, but after learning what terror hid inside the missing year of my childhood, a few unpaid bills hardly seemed to matter.

44

There were no games and little talking on the drive home. We only exchanged words when it came to practicalities, like stopping at service stations and discussing the best route to avoid traffic. Otherwise I turned inward and explored the warrens of my mind, seeing Theo grinning in his cheeky way for most of our childhood, happy and ready to face the world together... and then dark, as though he could turn to ash and blow away in the wind.

The comedown from whatever Paisley had dosed us with was making me feel less and less present, more and more like I was watching myself go through the motions.

I couldn't stop thinking about my son, nineteen years old, a fully grown man now.

He was out there. He needed me.

No, that was wrong.

If he thought about me at all, he probably resented the fact I'd given him away. I wondered if his parents had told him he was adopted.

I gave Freddy directions to Mum's house and we sat outside for a few minutes, weary from travel. Freddy blew out a short breath and smiled over at me, but there was sadness in his normally cheeky eyes. 'Do you want me to wait at yours or give you some space? You were in quite a state last night, and...'

'And what?' I took his hand, squeezing it tightly.

'Something's going on. Maybe you're freaked about the headstone, about Kayden. Maybe it's something else. But whatever it is, I'm here for you.'

I leaned over and brushed my lips against his cheek. I didn't have it in me to kiss him fully, passionately. 'You can wait at mine. I'll get a taxi back. I'm not sure how long I'll be. Unless *you* want space?'

'And leave my girlfriend to go through this alone?' His grin returned, lighting something inside of me.

Then the baby's innocent face snuffed it out.

I sensed the question within the question, and I tried my best to mirror his smile. 'You really are a great boyfriend, Freddy.'

I recalled my suspicions from the morning: that Freddy was the man in the hockey mask. I pushed them away. They were remnants of the drugs, nothing more, paranoia and fear unrooted in reality.

Climbing from the car, I approached my childhood home.

45

Mum blinked away tears when she opened the door. I found myself blurry-eyed too, memories of our argument stabbing at me. I rushed forward and wrapped my arms around her. 'Oh, Mum. I'm sorry. I shouldn't have shouted at you.'

'Hush.' She squeezed me tightly. 'What I said, it was unforgivable. I'm sorry, Eleanor. For everything.'

We went into the garden and Mum made us some tea. For a while we sat silently and watched butterflies dancing in the air, listening to the buzz of insects. One of the neighbour's cats sprung down from the fence, a gorgeous jet-black beauty with startling yellow eyes. It glanced at us, tilted its head, and then leapt away.

I glanced at Mum. She was fiddling with the knot on her bandana. 'Mum, I remembered what happened when I was a kid.'

Her hands paused. They dropped. 'You *remembered*, how?'

'It doesn't matter. But it's true, isn't it? I had a child with Theo. And we gave him away.'

'Did Georgia tell you?'

'Mum.' Bitterness snapped into my voice. 'I haven't once mentioned your overdue bills. It's clear you don't want to tell me what's going on. I only think it's fair you give me the same respect.'

'It's true,' she said. 'It's difficult for me to think about that time, your pregnancy. I was... well, I wasn't the greatest mother in the world.'

'This isn't about that. And you were great in some ways, really. We had some wonderful times together.'

'Thank you, thank you for saying that, but... Well, in any case. Theo's parents were determined for him not to ruin his life by having a child. I met with them several times to discuss it. I'm ashamed to say they convinced me rather easily. There were talks of an abortion, but you wouldn't hear it. You couldn't stand the idea.'

Kayden had murdered that idealistic part of me, that maternal part, whatever it was. I'd chosen an abortion for my second pregnancy because it was preferable to the alternative: to what our son would become if Kayden raised him, or the horrors he might commit if we had a daughter.

'After the birth, you unravelled. When I found you on the verge of committing suicide, I think something snapped in me. For the first time in a decade, I stopped looking *into* myself, I stopped, oh... I was always so *me-me-me*, wasn't I? I was always focused on myself. But the image of my daughter, my only child prepared to end her life...'

She dabbed at her cheeks with the sleeves of her billowing summer shirt. I remained where I was, transfixed, offering neither comfort nor solace.

'I called an ambulance and then I had no choice but to sort myself out. I did what I should have done in the months after your dear father's death. I pulled myself together. It was too late, much too late. And then you fell into that waking coma, and I was so scared, Ellie, terrified you'd never come back.'

'And when I did, and you realised I remembered nothing, you thought it was better not to tell me what had happened.'

'Why should we? You were ready to get on with your life. If you'd asked, of course we would have told you.'

'But I never asked. I preferred to be kept in the dark.'

'Exactly.'

'Do we know anything about him, my son?'

Mum shook her head. 'We thought it would be best to sever ties. It would be easier for everybody involved. I'm not sure how true that was, but that was our thinking.'

More tears stung my eyes. More sobs were trying to surge up my throat. I fought them both away. 'He was beautiful, Mum. His little face, the way he smiled up at me. He was ready for me to be his mother.'

'Oh, Ellie. There's still time. There's always time.'

I thought about Freddy, my supportive boyfriend. Perhaps we could have a family one day. 'I hope so.'

46

I have thought many times over the years about why Kayden wanted to have a family with me, why it seemed like he needed one. Honestly, I was not somebody to whom he should have wanted to tether himself. I think I have adequately demonstrated that in the preceding pages. I was broken and selfish and mad; mad most of all.

I have done unforgivable things.

I am getting tangled up in the telling. This is difficult for me to write about.

I have met with Kayden several times after that summer, of course. When he was married to my daughter – oh, God, poor Ellie, poor sweet innocent Ellie – he would often visit me, grinning at me from the doorway. 'Hello, mother-in-law. I've brought you some flowers.'

It was during one of these meetings he bluntly told me what Paisley had done to him as a child. He'd referenced it obliquely during the summer we met, and of course, I had my mind-reading delusion. But he had never stated it in unequivocal terms. What I mean to say is this: I knew, of course I knew what had been happening to him, but it was one of those ethereal truths that hover at the edge of everything. Even the images which swelled sickly in my mind were unknown to him, for – I believed – he did not know I had accessed that particular part of his past. Only much later I would remember the real truth.

I knew his mother had abused him, almost from the start, but he was always cagey about the issue. Understandably so.

But once, he visited me when he was very clearly drunk, face drained from crying. I opened the door and he collapsed against me. I had no choice but to hold him as he wept, seeming like a child even if we were both too ancient for this.

He cried as I sat him down and rubbed his shoulder, trying to comfort him. If I'd known what he was doing to Ellie... but can I really say I would have intervened? Kayden has become skilled at playing on my emotions, skilled at instilling fear within me, skilled at making me feel like I owe him.

And I do. I did. I owed him. I owe him.

He cried and said, 'She raped me, Lottie. There, there's the truth, in plain fucking English. My own mother raped me for years and there was nothing I could do about it and I felt weak and I felt pathetic and I never felt like a man after that, never. I couldn't after what that evil bitch did to me. But I love her. I still love her. She's my mum. How does that make any sense?'

But our argument, the summer I was young and he was younger... I was going to write about our argument, wasn't I?

He wanted us to have a family. He got very upset when I told him I wouldn't risk afflicting my children with my madness.

I asked him in the years after why he had been so determined to have children with me, but he would never give me a straight answer. The closest he ever got was looking me dead in the eye in that unnerving way of his, like he would happily kiss a person before killing them, and saying, 'A second chance, Lottie. Everyone deserves one. But it's too late anyway.'

That summer, I held the power. I was in charge.

(Pah! Pah! Pah!)

When he brought it up, I screamed at him to stop, to stop talking and to go and find some gullible slut to impregnate if he cared that much. I threw viciousness at him, so much of it he ended up backed against the wall, tears budding in his eyes. I ran over to him and I raked my fingernails down his naked chest – we'd just had sex – and I told him if he ever brought it up again, I would kill him.

He slapped me, hard. I fell to the floor and laughed, imagining the impact spreading through my body, turning to fire and fairies and myriad other mad things. And the Other cackled and clapped its hands together, over and over, each reverberation like a powerful gust of wind smashing through the house.

Staring up at him, I smiled, cackling as he stooped down to help me up.

I scratched at his face when he apologised, and he grimaced and hit me again. That could've been when he discovered how much he enjoyed inflicting pain upon women, imagining they were his mother each time he struck them, each time he made them squeal. He loomed over me for a moment, fists clenched, and something seemed to darken within him, as though the last of his boyhood had seeped out of his body.

That was the only time he ever led our sex, pouncing upon me as the violence turned to lust, as we ravaged each other. It was the only time – I remember this distinctly – he was on top, rutting like a possessed thing, and he climaxed far quicker than he usually did.

Our relationship was so malformed and wrong that afterward we held each other and talked of our star-bright future even as his body was flecked with blood from my overeager fingernails. We agreed to table the children discussion, and we talked about leaving together at the end of the summer, once I'd finished my novel: the novel I never started.

'I can't wait to start our life together, Lottie. It's the only thing keeping me going.'

The next bit hurts. But it will hurt more if I keep it stowed away inside of me. I cannot hide amongst my plants forever. I have to strip my mind bare of the weeds which have coiled around me, trapping me, stifling. Killing: a slow death that has taken decades and, I think, may have contributed to my second mental breakdown.

Here I am again, getting tangled, making no sense.

It is time I told the complete truth about what I did to Kayden Hunter.

47

I felt like I was living inside a glass box for the next few weeks. Life went on around me and I said and did everything I needed to, but most of the time I was dwelling on the image of my boy gazing up at me. Even the ranting customers at work had little effect. It seemed dim compared to the startling brightness of what I'd remembered.

Life, as it always does, kept going despite how I felt.

My book was released and I utterly failed in my promotion responsibilities. I'd had plans of running giveaways and taking a day off work so I could interact with my readers – and potential readers – on social media.

But with the negative reviews sitting on my page, and with my son's eyes watching me every moment of every day, I couldn't bring myself to care.

It was wrong. It was self-indulgent. It was precisely the sort of behaviour I'd promised myself I wouldn't devolve into, but I couldn't stop.

I'd aborted one child and given the other away.

The guilt gnawed relentlessly.

I almost sent Theo messages on Facebook a few times,

typing out whole essays about how I'd remembered and asking if he'd meet to discuss it. But there was nothing to discuss. All this had happened over a decade ago. It wasn't his fault it had only just arisen in my mind.

Luckily, Paisley seemed to have calmed down with her games. There were no pervert callers at work, no homeless accusers, no bricks through my window and no hockey-mask man. Perhaps drugging us had been her grand finale, the topper to her twisted games.

I was thankful not to see Kayden again. He neither peered at me from darkened glass nor stared at me in vivid daylight. He only gazed at me in my night terrors, a vicious grin peeling across his lips.

The police still had no leads on the man in the hockey mask.

The more time passed, the more convinced I became Paisley had hired somebody to attack me. I knew I should have gone to the police and told them, but then they would ask me why, and I'd be forced to explain about Kayden, about the abuse, about his suicide. I didn't want to drag it up, especially since things had seemed to calm down.

I was moving on.

Freddy was the only person who was able to make me feel anything during that walled-in period.

We would spend the evenings lying in bed together, Freddy on his laptop with the headphones on, tinkering on his music-editing app, as I lost myself in books I'd read dozens of times before. I needed comfort reads: worlds in which to disappear so I didn't have to think about the one I was living in.

Or we'd make love, slower and more caring than our first hungry exchanges, staring into each other's eyes as we climaxed.

Once, I shed tears toward the end, hot and brimming with bittersweet pleasure. Freddy paused and kissed the tears from my cheeks, making my skin tingle.

'It's okay, Ells. It's going to be okay.'

Was it okay, or was it *going* to be okay?

Because they were very different things and I couldn't believe the former. I couldn't believe how I felt was acceptable in any way, because I was so numb, so disconnected, thinking about my boy and not much else.

I obsessed about where he was and what he was doing with his life. I had no way of finding out. And if I did, I knew it would be unfair to spring up and try to claim that which I'd given away. My hope was he was in university studying something he was truly passionate about, that he was on a good track in life and making his way in the world. But as long as he was healthy and happy, living like any carefree nineteen-year-old boy, that would be enough for me.

'Are you all right, Ells?' Freddy murmured one night in bed, as I rested my cheek against his bare chest, eyes closed so I could focus on the sensation of his heartbeat.

'Why do you ask?'

'I guess you seem sort of... distant. I know you've been through a lot. But I swear, if that prick in the hockey mask ever comes back, I'll kill him. I promise you I'll kill him.'

I kissed his chest. 'No. You'd go to prison. And I need you here.'

He smoothed his hand over my shoulder, sensation tingling. 'Don't worry. I'm not going anywhere.'

That was our last pure moment: the final seconds of unmarred perfection before it unravelled. Soon he rose to take a shower, and his phone started to vibrate from the bedside table.

48

I remembered when we first started seeing each other, how a strange look had come across his face when his phone rang. I glanced at the bedroom door, listening for the shower, to make sure he wouldn't catch me snooping.

It wasn't the sort of thing trusting girlfriends were supposed to do.

But the phone *kept* vibrating.

Or, rather, it would vibrate, there was a pause, and then it would vibrate again.

Somebody was sending him text after text after text.

Who? What did they want?

I turned the phone over and stared at the screen. I couldn't unlock it – I didn't know his passcode – but I could see snippets of the texts in the notifications window. They came in almost too fast for me to read, all from a contact called Joe's Pizza. It was clearly a fake name.

I stared, a hole opening in my gut, sucking away thoughts of a future with Freddy.

I'd done it again.

I was an idiot.

I'd trusted the wrong fucking man *again*.

You have to tell her.
Don't make me force you.
I will rape her in front...
I will end you both.
TELL. HER. THE. TRUTH.

'Ellie.' I spun to find Freddy standing in the doorway, a towel wrapped around his waist. 'What are you doing?'

He asked the question as a reflex, but I could hear the resignation in his voice. He knew what I'd seen. He knew I'd caught him. I just had no clue what I'd caught him doing. 'What do you need to tell me? What is going on? The truth... what truth?'

49

He walked across the room, reaching out to me with the hand that wasn't clasped onto his towel. I shifted around him, pressing myself almost flat against the wall, desperate to get as far away from him as possible.

You have to tell her.

My breath was coming far too quickly, threatening to bring a panic attack crashing down on me.

'Ells, calm down–'

I wheeled on him. '*Don't* fucking call me Ells and *don't* fucking tell me to calm down. What the hell is going on?'

He dropped onto the bed, pressing his hands together in his lap. He stared at the floor, glanced at me – with eyes that tried to melt me – and then back at the floor. 'I don't know where to start.'

'How about at the beginning?' I walked over to the wardrobe and grabbed some jogging bottoms and a hoodie.

'What are you doing?'

'I don't like being half-naked in front of strangers.' I forcefully pulled on the bottoms, glaring at him, and then quickly pulled the hoodie over my head. 'Explain, Freddy. Now.'

'I love you, Ellie. That's the truth.'

'No.' I moved over to the door, one foot over the threshold, ready to dart away if I needed to. 'If you loved me, you wouldn't be keeping secrets from me.'

'Why are you standing like that?' Tears glimmered in his eyes. His voice cracked. He looked young and stupid and handsome. 'I'm not going to hit you.'

'I can't put anything past you.'

'That's not fair.'

'The. Fucking. Truth.'

'We can talk about this, but it doesn't have to... There's something real here, Ells. Even if I've made some mistakes.'

I stared at him, doing my best to keep my breathing under control. Freddy had been the one bright spot in my life after the revelation of my teenage pregnancy: the warm body in my bed to stave off the cold of everything else. 'What mistakes?'

He ran a hand through his shower-wet hair. 'It started with a text. It came from an anonymous number. It told me to go to a café and there'd be some cash waiting for me behind the counter. That's it. Go to a café, pick up some cash. The text said it was a present. I thought... fuck it. What do I have to lose? Maybe one of my mates was playing a trick on me. But when I got there, there was two hundred quid waiting for me. And a note: *This proves I'm serious. Await further instructions*.'

I leaned heavily against the wall. 'What instructions?'

'There was a phone call next. I guess this person got my phone number off my band's website, Facebook... It's on lots of places online. Anyway, the phone call came through–'

'Was it a man or a woman?'

It could've been Paisley. It could've been Kayden. They were the only two people I could imagine doing this to me.

'They were using a voice changer. I still have no idea who it is.'

'Why should I believe you?' He scowled at me, and for a second I honestly considered leaping across the room and driving my thumbnails into his eye sockets. 'Don't fucking look at me like that. You're the one in the wrong here.'

'I'm telling you the truth.' He sulked. 'I have no idea who this person is, only that they pay, they keep paying.'

'So what did they say on the phone?'

'That I should move to Weston and apply for a job at FCA. When I told them I had no experience, they said they'd gotten some dirt on the head honcho there. Nigel. He's been cheating on his wife and this person had video evidence of it, I guess.'

Freddy had *always* gotten special treatment, and I'd never understood why. I felt stupid. But how could I have guessed something so deranged?

'You blackmailed Nigel to get a job.'

'Yes.'

'But why?'

A solitary tear slid down his cheek. He pawed at it angrily. 'They told me to bide my time, and then, when the moment was right – when they instructed me to, I mean...'

'Jesus fucking *Christ*, Freddy.' My mind unpicked every moment of the past few weeks, every stupid, romantic, naïve moment, stripping it bare and revealing the maggots and the filth and the nastiness beneath. 'They instructed you to seduce me.'

He stared miserably. 'Yes.'

I'd known it the whole time, on some level: not the specifics, not about this twisted game. But I knew trusting him was a mistake, like trusting Kayden had been a mistake, like trusting any man after Theo had been a mistake. They promised the sun and delivered the barest flickering candle instead.

'And you went along with it. For the money.'

'Yes. But–'

I raged forward, waving my hand at him. 'But? *But?* There is no fucking *but* now, you bastard, you waste of fucking *breath.* Don't you get it? You've broken me, Freddy. I thought you were different.'

He rose, reaching out to me. His towel dropped and his cock hung there limply. He smirked at me as he reached for his towel, as though he'd forgotten for half a second I hated him. 'Sorry, Ells.'

'Shut the fuck up. Why?'

'Why what?'

'Why the fuck did they tell you to seduce me?' I raised my hand, the same way I had with Mum when we'd had our argument, but this time I wasn't able to stop myself.

I struck him across the face.

The flesh-on-flesh noise seemed too loud, and revoltingly it reminded me of sex, of the fleshy noises our bodies had made only hours previously. I retreated to the door, animal impulses screaming at me to get out of there before he retaliated.

But he only stared. 'I didn't ask questions. They told me to make you care about me. The money kept coming in. But then *I* started to care, Ells. I really started to care and...' He croaked and sobbed, and then he kept sobbing. It was like something burst in him as he stood there with one hand clasped on the towel and the other smothering his face. 'I fucking love you.'

I hated the reflex that tried to take possession of me, driving me across the room and into his arms: telling him we could fix this.

But we couldn't. Never.

'It must be Paisley, fucking Paisley. This is what she meant with those hints, those jabs. Maybe she and Kayden planned it before his death. But why would Kayden commit suicide before he got to see his plan come to fruition?'

My mind whirred as I turned away, worrying over the problem.

Learning of my childhood pregnancy had made me feel distant, so I weaponised that distance. I retreated from the moment and closed myself off from emotion. I wouldn't be pulled in by Freddy's pathetic crying. I wouldn't allow myself to care. I strode into the hallway and pulled on my shoes.

'Where are you going?'

'Away from you. I want you gone when I get home. We're done.'

'Wait–'

I left the flat and slammed the door behind me, the reverberation moving through the building, as though the whole thing could come crashing down. That would be fine by me. I couldn't live there anymore, not after the visions of Kayden and this: the destruction of the only unmarred thing in my life.

As I walked onto the street, a thought occurred to me, a thought that changed everything.

If Kayden was the one who had hired Freddy, he would've known we were going to Scotland to check his grave. He could've arranged a fake headstone after all.

50

I pulled my hoodie up and picked up my pace.

The evening was cloudy and cool and the hockey-mask man could appear any second.

As I walked, another question struck me, perhaps the most important of all.

Of all the men in the country, of all the possible candidates for this sadistic scheme, why had they picked Freddy?

There was only one place I could go: the place I could always go if I had a problem.

It took me almost an hour to walk to Mum's house, almost jogging down the main roads, flinching at every passing car and gust of wind. I'd forgotten my purse, so I didn't have any money for a taxi or the bus. I was thankful a remnant of sunlight was bleeding through the clouds, not completely set, making me able to believe I'd arrive safely even if the hockey-mask man had attacked me in daylight last time.

Finally I arrived. I walked up the lane and knocked.

There was shuffling, and then Mum pulled the door open.

At first I thought the red smear across her face was her bandana. I was used to seeing her wear one, blood-red, twilight-purple, sunrise-yellow, but then I peered closer and I saw the blood, streams of it, and her face dropped. 'Why did you have to come?'

'Mum.' I rushed forward. 'What happened? Why are you bleeding?'

'Because I hit her.'

It was the voice of the man who had roared at me when I overcooked his eggs, who had told me he loved me and always would and he'd never let anything happen to me, who'd growled at me to moan as he raped me.

Kayden strolled down the hallway, casually tossing a knife from hand to hand, the hilt offensively wet with my mother's blood. He grinned. 'Hello, dear wife.'

51

I will always remember the way he hammered on the door that morning. I awoke with the certainty the hammering was coming from deep in the earth, that any moment an earthquake would rend its way through the house, through me, and I would split in half. At first I felt sure it was the Other, and I did what I usually did when she arrived, even if experience should have taught me by then it wouldn't work. I hid.

I scurried across the room and threw myself under the desk. I pressed my head between my knees and squeezed them tightly, trying to blot out the sound.

Voices whispered at me from every direction, taunting, mocking.

'There are going to be two Lotties,' they hissed. 'And neither of them is good enough. Do the world a favour and get rid of them both. Go on. You can do it. You can end it with one quick razor-blade kiss.'

The hammering went on – the voices got louder – and then I realised they were coming from the source of the noise: outside the house, outside the window.

'Get out here, you sick bitch. Get the fuck out here *now*.'

I slid out from my place and crept over to the window. I remained crouched, certain a projectile was going to smash the glass and slam into me, puncturing me, killing me.

But I had to see if the voice came from one of my people – one of the characters who visited me in the forest – or from one of *those* people. I know how deranged this distinction was. At least it was not the Other, for facing her was worse than all of it.

There were real and pretend people. That was all.

Kayden's father, Delaney, stood in the tangled garden beneath my bedroom window. The sight of him has branded itself into my mind, the weeds and the vines and the rioting nature out of control, his chest heaving, his fists clenched.

'I see you. Get the fuck down here. We need to talk.'

'About what?' I yelled at him. 'Go away.'

'No chance. You raped my son. You abused my only fucking *child*. Come down here or I'm going to call the police.'

His words made no sense to me then. When I looked back at what Kayden and I had shared, I saw the purity, the beauty of it. I felt his fingers moving through my hair and his body pressed against mine. I felt the love.

'Now,' Delaney shouted, he kept shouting. He wouldn't stop. 'Or I'll kick the fucking door in. I swear to God.'

'Where is Kayden?'

'Never mind that, you slag. Get down here.'

One of my chief fears back then was being taken away by *them*, whoever they were, so they could torture my book idea out of me. I had no book idea and nobody cared about me, but I still couldn't stand the idea of the police charging in with their batons and their teeth and their hate.

Rape.

I wasn't a rapist. That was impossible, wasn't it?

I opened the door and Delaney exploded into the hallway. He was a huge man and I shrunk from him, my hands rising defensively over my face, letting out a screech that made me feel weak, not at all like the powerful empress I had tricked myself into believing I was.

'Stop it,' he said to me. 'I'm not going to hit you. But I should. I'm giving you a chance, you psychotic slut. Leave tonight and never come back. Never fucking *think* about coming back. My wife and my boy don't want the police called. God knows why. But there it is.'

I knew why Paisley did not want the police called about anything. I have made clear in these pages what she did to Kayden. I had read his mind and seen it all. That was how I *thought* I knew.

'You said rape.' I waved my finger at him. 'I would never do such a disgusting thing.'

He walked right up to me, bringing with him the stink of sweat, the presence of rage. He stopped only when his chest was almost crushing my face and pressing the back of my head against the wall.

I gazed into his eyes and I knew – in my mind-reading way – he'd killed people before and he would again. I have no clue if this is true. In fact, I very much doubt it. But that's what I thought as I stared up at him.

'My son is fifteen years old. He has scratches all over his body and I found him in tears last night. It took me hours to work the truth out of him. You forced him to bring you food. You lured him here. You had sex with him against his will. You physically assaulted him.'

'You're wrong. He's eighteen. Kayden is eighteen.'

Delaney slammed the wall near my head, and upstairs I heard somebody skitter across the landing, one of my characters getting ready to pick my corpse apart when he was done with me. 'Are you telling me I don't know how old my fucking *son* is?'

I cringed away from him. 'Where is he?'

'Do you think I'm going to let you anywhere near him?'

'Dad.' Kayden strode into the room. Blood poured from his eyes, rivers of it, gaping crimson holes where his startling blues used to be. I blinked and the blood became tears. The redness was from crying. He looked like he did after we had sex sometimes.

How did I not make that connection? Why had I never questioned his tears?

I was ill, but it's no excuse. Most people with my affliction would never dream of taking advantage the way I did. And the other excuses, the pity-me excreta with which I could fill these pages – I do not deserve them, I have never deserved them. A person must stand by their actions.

'Don't hit her, Dad. It's not... as simple as you think.'

'You're a child, Kayden.'

'The sex is separate from everything else.' He let out a sob that became a crackling croaking noise. I was certain he was going to collapse and die right there, and I ducked under Delaney's arm and ran at my lover, my victim.

'No you don't.' Delaney grabbed my wrist and threw me to the floor. He loomed over me, his shadow making my skin cold. 'If you try to touch him again, I will beat you into the fucking grave.'

'Kayden. Tell him the truth. Please tell him the truth.'

'You know the truth.' Kayden moved up next to his father, his hands clawing at his face. I silently screamed for him to stop: stop it now, or he'd peel away his lovely skin. 'Stop pretending.'

But I had no clue what he was talking about. I swear on my sweet Ellie's life I had no idea.

The memories would return to me in violent flashes over the coming weeks. I recalled nothing in the immediate aftermath.

But I can see it now, in hateful vivid detail.

~

I had wiped so much from my mind. I had erased the evil words I'd hissed in his ear when he begged me to stop. 'If you try to tell anyone, I'll send those photos to everybody in your school. Everybody will see what a tiny pathetic little prick you have. You'll have to run away, you cunt. Get on your knees and do what you're fucking told.'

I said those words: I hurled them at him.

And the crying – the way he cried when we had sex – it was because he didn't want it. He'd pushed me away the first time I tried to initiate it with him, pawing at him, and then I'd cried and called him a monster, a woman-beater.

He'd knelt next to me. He'd pleaded with me. 'I didn't mean to hurt you. What can I do, Lottie? I'm sorry.'

Oh, God...

Why did I do this?

When he asked me what he could do, I pushed him onto the floor and I pulled his trousers down and I took his fifteen-year-old cock in my mouth and I sucked it, and I felt how it was hateful to him, and I kept sucking until his animal responses kicked in. And then the tears had started, as I rode him, as I painted his chest in brutal nail marks.

'See,' I said afterward, kissing the tears from his cheek. 'You like it. Tell Lottie you like it.'

His voice, numb, will always be with me: 'I like it.'

'Good boy.'

Boy, boy, boy.

I'd invented the moment when he told me he was eighteen. There wasn't much wrong with a woman of twenty-three years and a man of eighteen being together, but twenty-three and fifteen, a woman and a child, a confused child at that? I'd invented it – or, but no, there is no *or*. I refuse absolution. I cannot make excuses.

I raped him.

I abused him.

I manipulated him.

There was reality mixed in with the fiction. I'd twisted the poor boy's mind to the point where he truly wished to run away with me, perhaps because I'd shown him some paltry kindness amidst the torment, perhaps because being raped by me was preferable to being raped by his mother.

I'd erased so many evil moments.

I tied him by his hands to the rafters, so he could only graze the floor with the tips of his toes, stripped him naked and spent hours and hours committing all manner of perversions on him.

I collected every cylindrical object in the house to see if they'd fit inside of him.

I burnt his skin with matches.

I pissed on him.

I forced him to become hard as I hissed in his face, 'You're fucking wrong, you're fucking broken. You really *enjoy* this shit?'

On and on and on, I'd done so much to him, and then pushed it down deep, beneath my unconquerable ego, beneath my supposed genius.

But when I begged Kayden to tell his father the truth, I truly believed the fiction I'd invented.

Kayden shook his head. 'Lottie, please. Please. We can move past this if you're honest.'

'Fuck's sake, Kay. Listen to yourself. You should be trying to kill this bitch.'

'But I love her, Dad–'

Delaney's fist smashed into his son's face. Kayden flew across the room, tripping over his feet, landing with a violent bone-crunching noise on the floor. 'Never say that again. Never *think* that.' He turned to me. 'You see what you've done? If you're still here at the end of the day, I'm rounding up the boys and we're going to do some real damage to you.'

Delaney grabbed his son and dragged him to his feet, turning and pulling him toward the door. Kayden dropped a piece of paper before he disappeared through the threshold.

I stayed where I was until all I could hear was the creaking in the house and the familiar voices buried within them, and then I scurried over to the note and unfolded it.

Please take me with you, Lottie. We can still make this work. I love you, even if you've made mistakes.

And my response to his words?

There was no shame.

I was so wrapped up in the belief I had done nothing wrong. The self-hate and the gnawing guilt would come only later, once I truly realised what I'd done.

Staring down at his note, it was the word *mistakes* that bit into me.

How dare he tell me *I'd* made mistakes when he was the one who'd lied to his father about his age, about our relationship?

It made no sense. Of course Delaney knew his son's age, but it didn't need to make sense for me to believe it.

This was a trick to reach into my mind and steal my novel idea: the novel that never existed.

That – and not the magnitude of what I'd done – was why I decided to leave the village and never return.

52

I backed away from him, instinct driving me, but he darted
forward and grabbed Mum by the back of her hair. She let
out a wail as he brought the knife to her throat, that sick grin
smeared across his face: the grin that had haunted me every day
of my life since we separated. 'Don't be stupid, Ellie. Come on.
Let's have a chat.'

Mum was limp within his grasp. She didn't fight, just stood
there with an empty look in her eyes.

I had no choice.

I walked into the house and closed the door behind me,
wondering if this could possibly be another apparition.

'I guess you're not dead then.' My voice was dull.

Kayden giggled in a childlike way. 'You're still not sure? Jesus,
Ellie, you really are a mental fucking cunt, aren't you?'

He dragged Mum toward the living room, nodding at me to
follow. I walked on dreamish legs, feeling as though I was
floating as I walked through the door and over to the sofa. I sat
down and folded my arms across myself. With Kayden's hands
on my mother there was nothing I could do, no way to fight
back.

Kayden slid into the armchair and pulled Mum into his lap, his arm coiled around her waist, the knife casually pressed against her side.

'You arranged it all. The customers at work, the reviews, the homeless man on the beach. You were the man in the hockey mask. You pushed me into the pond. You threw a brick through my window.'

Kayden nodded hungrily, his eyes vivid with pleasure. It was a look I recognised well: the look he gave me when he was inflicting pain. 'Yes.'

I gestured at Mum, fighting off a sob. 'Please let her go.'

'You should be angry with her. She's the one who's been paying my way all these years. She paid for me to bribe those reviewers. She paid for my fake headstone.'

I thought about the bills: the way Mum had snapped at me. Kayden had been stealing her money.

But why would Mum give him anything?

'She's done nothing to deserve this,' I whispered.

Mum let out a jagged gulping sob, like she was drowning, and Kayden laughed maniacally. 'Is that so, Lottie? Are you innocent in this?'

'Oh, God...' Mum trembled. 'Please, please don't do this.'

'Shut up. You were the one stupid enough to write it down. I didn't force you, did I?'

'I couldn't live with it, in my head, always there. The regret. Please.'

I looked between them. There was something happening, something strange and wrong. Kayden and Mum had met a few times during our marriage, and Kayden had always turned on his charm around her, smiling and playing the perfect son-in-law. It didn't make sense for them to be talking so intimately.

'What the fuck are you talking about?' I sat up. 'What regret?'

'Hang on.' Kayden reached into his pocket and took out his phone, aiming it at me. 'Smile, bitch.'

The camera shutter sound went off and he typed quickly.

'What are you doing?'

'I need to prove to lover boy you're really here. We can't have him missing out. In the meantime, why don't you do some light reading?' He nodded to the coffee table. A notebook sat atop it. The cover was crinkled as though it had been roughly handled: as though its owner had debated destroying it.

'I don't understand. Mum...'

'Ellie, my sweet beautiful wife, I will gut your cunt mother and rape you on her corpse if you don't do as you're told.'

He didn't speak with the savage intensity of a man trying to make me believe him. His words were matter-of-fact and true. I believed him completely.

So I reached for the notebook, as something deep inside screamed at me to stop, that reading these words could be more painful than the rest of it.

'God, no,' Mum whimpered as I turned the first page.

53

'This can't be true.' Tears burned my eyes as I closed the last page, the force of Mum's testimony making thinking difficult. I couldn't put any of it into order. 'So you raped him, Mum? You abused him? You... Oh, no, no, please, no.'

I threw the notebook across the room and buried my face in my hands. I cried for a long time as Mum let out moans and Kayden's giggles punctuated the sound of my ragged sobs. I cried as I went over her words: her psychosis, her delusions, and then the final sickening reveal of what she'd really done to him.

I collected every cylindrical object in the house to see if they'd fit inside of him. I burnt his skin with matches. I pissed on him.

The sentences stabbed into my mind, tearing holes that would never heal, no matter how long I lived.

So much of it had been nonsensical ranting: the voices, the *Other*, whatever the fuck that was supposed to mean. But the cold fact of her abuse was right there, laid out in grotesque detail.

'Why do you think I chose you, Ellie?' Kayden was high with glee. 'A mediocre-looking slut sitting on the seafront trying to look sophisticated. Look at you. You're nothing special. Maybe good for a few quick shags here and there, but to marry, to fall in love with? I'd rather fuck your rapist mother again. You got boring after a while. When you had your big moment – oh, you were so proud – I thought, fuck it, I'll go home and find somebody who isn't a sad sack woe-is-me cunt. It was nothing to do with your *bravery*.'

I dropped my hands, staring through the torrent of tears. 'Mum, tell me it's not true. Tell me he made you write this.'

She shook her head, her cheeks sunken. 'It's true. God help me, it's all true.'

'And you thought you could skip into your fresh new life, with your shit book nobody in their right mind will ever read. I couldn't let that happen. It was easy enough to use lovely Lottie's money to fund my campaign of madness. Hey, I quite like the sound of that... maybe I should write a book called *Campaign of Madness* once I'm done with you two.'

'But why target me?' I wiped at my cheeks. They stung. It hurt. 'I didn't rape you. I didn't do *anything* to you.'

His eyes were hazy for a moment. 'Because she...' And then he trailed off with a grin. 'Because it was so much better than our other games.' He stroked his hand over Mum's hair, smearing blood into the grey. Thankfully the cut had stopped bleeding, but there was still too much of it, sticky against her scalp. 'The way you looked at me that night, the uncertainty in your eyes. It was delicious.'

'And you hired Freddy. You wanted to make me love again only to wrench it away.'

He looked like he was about to burst with excitement. 'Is that all?'

'No. You told him to keep tabs on me. That's how you knew we were going to Scotland to visit your grave. I guess you found a gravesite nobody ever visited and replaced the stone.'

He threw his head back and laughed violently. Mum and I

exchanged a glance, but it was too messy for solidarity. I could never look at her as I once had: the woman who'd made a few mistakes but, ultimately, cared for me deep down. She'd known who Kayden was this entire time and she never said anything. She was an abuser.

'Please, please, *please*,' Kayden said, between titters, 'tell me you haven't guessed this last bit. Oh, God, please tell me you're that fucking stupid.'

'I don't understand.'

'Of course you don't. You were never as clever as you thought. You were–'

The doorbell cut through his sentence. The everyday sound didn't fit with the blood smeared across Mum's face and the pain in my gut.

'Must be lover boy.' Kayden stood and dragged Mum up by her arm, pausing to leer at me. 'I don't need to tell you what happens if you try anything, do I?'

I shook my head, feeling like prey. I hated it.

'Use your words, Ellie. And make sure to call me *sir* or I might have to cut this bitch.'

'No...' I almost spat at him, and I wouldn't care if it hit Mum instead. 'Sir.'

'Good girl. Come on, Lottie.'

He pulled her from the room.

54

I rose from the sofa as quietly as I could and crept across the room, to the small writing table in the corner. Praying that the drawer wasn't locked, I reached for the handle and pulled it slowly, ever so slowly because sometimes it made a creaking, scraping noise.

Freddy's voice rose. 'What the fuck is going on? Where's Ellie?'

'She's waiting for you. She's *very* excited to see you.'

I opened the drawer and reached inside, taking out the letter opener Mum stored in there. The handle was welcomingly cold against my sweaty skin, offering hope.

Tucking it into my hoodie's kangaroo pocket, I sneaked across the room and sat down gently.

I had no idea what I was going to do with it, how I'd get past Mum to use it on Kayden, but I felt better with it pressing through my clothes against my belly. Perhaps I could find a way to stab him, to lacerate his supercilious face, to stab and keep stabbing until there was nothing left but his insufferably captivating eyes, and maybe a few chunks of his silver hair... hair

I'd loved to run my fingers through at the beginning, memories which made me hate my old self.

'Ellie?' Freddy strode into the room, relief flooding into his face when he saw I was unharmed. He rushed over to me, looping his arm around me and squeezing me close. I hated him, but I leaned into the embrace anyway. He was warm and safe and all the things he'd been before I learned the truth. 'I'm so glad you're okay.'

'She's far from okay, young man.' Kayden swaggered in, shoving Mum into the armchair and standing behind it with the knife pointed at the back of her head. 'In fact, neither of you are. You're both incredibly fucking sick in the head.'

'How do you think this is going to end for you, mate?' Freddy wheeled on him, rising to his feet.

'Ah-ah, easy, tiger.' Kayden grabbed a fistful of Mum's hair and yanked it back. She yelped as her throat was exposed, baring her wrinkled skin. 'Or shall I open this paedo bitch up?'

I placed my hand on Freddy's back, grabbing his shirt and pulling him back onto the sofa. He sat down and let out a shivering breath. 'I've already told Ellie the truth. She knows you paid me, whoever the fuck you are.'

'I'm her husband.' Kayden beamed. 'And I, young man, am a genius.'

'Is that so?' Freddy's voice brimmed with familiar sarcasm. 'Doesn't take a genius to hold an old lady hostage. Takes a coward, but not a genius.'

Kayden's grin widened as he stared at me. I reached into my hoodie pocket, squeezing the hilt of the letter opener, my whole body tense with the need to use it. But Mum looked too tragic with her head bent backward. The noises she made were too terror-filled, tugging at parts of me which couldn't die even if I knew what she was, what she'd done. 'Have you really not worked it out yet?'

'Worked *what* out?' I snapped. 'You've played your game. You've–'

'Do you remember how you cried about that little gap in your memory, sweet wife? Do you remember how I held you, how I told you you weren't mad, oh no, you weren't mad at all. Do you?'

'Yes.' He'd offered me such sweet solace, holding me for the entire night, letting me cry myself to sleep. 'It was fake like everything was fake. Big fucking deal.'

'But it *is* a big deal. Because I knew what you'd forgotten. Lottie has found it difficult to say no to me over the years. You see, for somebody who'd abuse a child, she's really quite weak. Especially now she lives in boring old reality with the rest of us. Isn't that right?' He pulled roughly on her hair, forcing her to nod up and down. 'See? She agrees.'

'You're a coward,' I hissed. 'You're a fucking *mongrel*.'

'I knew you'd had a child... Tell her, Freddy.'

'Tell her what?' Freddy looked at me and then Kayden. 'I don't understand. You had a kid?'

'Tell her how old you are.'

I bolted to my feet and stared at him, my heartbeat cracking inside my chest. 'He's twenty-five. Nice try, you sick fuck.'

'Is that right?' Kayden beamed at Freddy. 'Is that how old you are?'

'You told me to lie about my age, you deranged psychopath.'

'So how old are you? It's a simple question.'

'I'm nineteen.'

55

I keeled over as my belly cramped, as vomit forced its way up my throat and spewed over my shoes and the carpet. My knees buckled and I puked more as though I could expel what Freddy and I had done from my body.

I collapsed onto my hands and knees and retched until I was empty, hollowed-out.

This was it: what Paisley had hinted at.

It wasn't that Freddy had been hired to seduce me.

This was why they'd picked him.

'Please no,' I gasped. 'Please fucking God *no*.'

'Ellie, Jesus...' Freddy knelt beside me, putting his hand on my shoulder. I lashed out, slapping him, needing to get him as far away from me as possible. 'What the *fuck* is going on?'

'You really are a moron, aren't you, kid?' Kayden chuckled. 'You're adopted.'

'Yeah, I'm adopted, so what... No, no, fucking no.'

'Yes, yes,' Kayden sang, 'fucking *yes*.'

I fell onto my side, my breathing acidic and burning from the vomit, my mind replaying the moments I'd shared with

Freddy, the intimacy: the sex and the laughter and the kissing and the belief he might be the man to finally make it all better.

'Ellie is your mother. You hear that, sweet wife? You fucked your own son. And you say *I'm* the sick one.'

56

'You're a fucking liar!' I screamed, leaping to my feet and moving toward Kayden.

He dragged Mum to her feet by her hair, eliciting a warbling cry that went right to my centre, to the piece of me which had sworn to always protect her and keep her safe ever since I was a little girl. Nothing else would've stopped me – the sickness of what he'd done was too great – but that did.

I paused, rubbing at the vomit coating my lips.

'I used the money Lottie kindly provides to hire a private investigator and find the mite. He was working in a bar and trying to get his dog-shit band a record deal. He's quite like you in that way, Ellie, with his mediocre talents. But, of course, you would be similar.'

Freddy was standing beside me, rage emanating from him. I could feel the heat but I dare not look at him. Because then I might throw myself at him instead of Kayden, bury my thumbs in his eyes, do whatever it took to make him go away forever. It wasn't fair. It wasn't his fault Kayden was deranged.

'When's your birthday, Freddy?' Kayden went on, his grin never faltering.

Freddy whispered the date: the same date I'd given my child away.

I paced up and down the room, my hands in my hair, tugging at it so hard several pieces came loose and my scalp stung. But it was easier than thinking about what we'd done together, the sex, the *sex*.

I'd had multiple orgasms with my own son.

I'd thought to myself, *Fuck, he's good, he's so good*.

And he was my son.

He was my son.

'No, no, no, no.' I wept then collapsed against the chair. My heartbeat was too frantic. I choked and struggled to breathe. 'It can't be. It can't be. It can't be.'

'But it is.' Kayden leaned down and brought his face close to Mum. She was staring off into space, her eyes glassy, the same way I must've looked in my waking coma when I blotted Freddy's existence from my mind. 'Do you see what you've done, Lottie? You thought you could skip off into a nice *normal* life. But look. Look at where it got you. This is your punishment for what you did. This is the price you pay. The past always catches up. Always. You were never safe. We were waiting.'

I rubbed my legs up and down over and over. I couldn't sit still. There was too much pain scorching through me.

I knew I'd never love again. I knew I'd never be able to look at myself in the mirror. I might take a razor blade to my wrist when the agony of this perversion crushed too heavily.

If I got out of there alive.

I wasn't sure I wanted to.

'My son. My child.'

'Your son.' Kayden laughed. 'Your child.'

'He's lying.' I could feel Freddy staring at me from his place near the sofa, but I refused to turn to him. I'd vomit again if I had to meet his intense gaze. 'Ellie. You didn't have a baby, did you?'

'I did. And I gave him away. On your birthday.'

'I have proof,' Kayden said cheerfully. 'Hang on. I'll email it to you. If I decide to let you go, you can peruse it at your leisure.'

He reached into his pocket and took out his phone. He must've had the email saved, because he only had to tap a few times before dropping it back into his pocket. My phone vibrated against my leg, but I didn't reach for it. I believed him without the proof.

The dates matched.

I'd fucked my son.

My son.

I'd fucked my fucking son.

The enormity started to work its way through Freddy. His breath was loud, ramping up through his clenched teeth, as though he was about to explode in a fury of violence.

'Look, Lottie, your daughter and your grandson. Look what you did to them. Look what you fucking *did*–'

Mum screamed as she leapt away from him, spinning and slapping him across the face. There was a loud *tear* as strands of her hair came loose in his hand, and then she ducked and ran across the room.

I didn't think.

I was sick and I didn't care if I died, as long as Kayden died too, as long as he got what he deserved.

I jumped and ran at him, pulling the letter opener from my pocket.

Kayden cackled and backhanded me across the face, making it seem far too easy.

I crashed into the floor. My bones shook.

And then he was on me, his breath hot against my face, the

same way it'd been countless times during our marriage. 'Have it your way.'

He brought the knife to my throat.

57

The knife kissed my skin coldly.

Part of me willed him to apply more pressure, to keep pushing until it plunged deeply and I didn't have to live with the perversion I'd committed. But my body responded as my mind lost hope. I brought the letter opener toward his side, meaning to stab him, to hurt him as he'd hurt me countless times.

Freddy looped his arm around Kayden's neck and dragged him to his feet. For what felt like several torturous minutes – but was truly only half a breath – I stared at the sight of my son with his arm around my resurrected husband's neck. Freddy's face was twisted in rage, his eyes blazing, and for a hateful second I remembered how he'd looked once when we were having sex: that same rage, that same obsessive expression.

My *son.*

I rolled away, panting, touching my neck to see if Kayden had done any damage. Which was a stupid thing to check for. He'd already hurt me more than he ever could.

I didn't know how to feel when I found my skin unharmed. It would've been easier if he'd slit me open, let torrents of blood gush down my body: the body I'd thrown against Freddy's, grinding his length, bouncing and moaning with no clue we shared, we shared–

Everything, we shared everything. He was the boy at the heart of this.

Finally, time resumed, and Freddy spun Kayden around.

'Fucking animal.' He headbutted Kayden so hard he flew across the room, smashing into the wall. 'Fucking *monster*.'

Kayden threw himself forward, trying to bring the knife in a wide arc toward Freddy, but the younger man – my son, my strong, beautiful, broken baby boy – was far too fast.

He rushed him and smashed his shoulder into his chest, tackling him to the floor and then falling upon him.

The attack was feral.

I could only sit there, paralysed, as Freddy entered a state of pure fury.

He punched Kayden in the face over and over, the sound like a baseball bat hitting a piece of meat, throwing his whole body into the strikes. Mum was suddenly behind me, her hands on my shoulders, helping me to stand and pulling me away from the violence.

Kayden brought the knife up into Freddy's side, burying it deep, a blossom of vivid red spreading through his shirt.

But nothing could stop Freddy. He punched and punched until Kayden's arms fell slack, until his body began to twitch and reverberate in death throes.

He kept on, crushing Kayden's nose into his face, his cheeks swelling to twice, and then three times their regular size.

Minutes passed and Freddy kept going.

Finally, the paralysis which had gripped me fell away.

I stared in full horror at what was happening, at what *I* had done. I couldn't stop thinking it was my fault, over and over, on a hissing loop in my mind: *all your fault all your fault all your fault.* Because I should've known, the moment I saw him, that Freddy belonged to me. I should've remembered those hopeful eyes and those lips and the feel of his skin against mine.

Freddy's breathing became laboured and the room filled with the stink of blood and shit and piss, as Kayden voided himself in death, and Freddy wouldn't stop. On and on, he brought his blood-smeared fists down against Kayden's face.

A triumphant part of me sang as Freddy unleashed himself on Kayden's corpse. My mum's hand on my shoulder felt very far away, numb, everything numb. And yet there were whole worlds writhing and boiling beneath the veil of numbness.

One part urged me to dart forward and join in: to peel away Kayden's skin and force it down his throat, to cut off his rapist's cock and shove it into his eye socket. Macabre and evil vignettes blazed in my mind, sending tingles over my body, willing me to leap on his face with both my feet, crush his jaws, crush his soul.

But it was my baby boy who was inflicting this damage, my beautiful, precious baby boy, the one they'd taken from me, the one they'd said I was too young and immature to take care of. Yet look what had become of us without each other's love. I never would've fallen for Kayden if I'd had my Theo, my Freddy, the life I should've fought with every last breath to protect.

This part of me screamed it wasn't too late. We could salvage this. He could still be my bundle of joy.

What a fucking joke.

'Evil.' Freddy hit Kayden. 'Piece of.' He hit him. 'Shit.' He hit him.

I took a step forward, hand outstretched, but I couldn't bring myself to touch Freddy. To touch him would mean to feel his flesh against mine, the confusing warmth, awakening yet another piece of me: the piece which refused to believe he was mine, refused to believe I'd committed one of the most reprehensible acts imaginable.

I let my hand drop and gawped at the bloody mess he'd made.

Kayden's face had exploded in a torrent of gore and it spread around him, sinking into the carpet, splattering Freddy's face so he became a picture of carnage.

'Freddy.' My voice was as distant and numb as everything else. I must've seemed strangely calm, even as my insides were twisting and my fingers twitching for the blade. I'd slice myself open like I tried to as a teenager, but this time I'd do it right: hit the right place, let it all pour out. 'That's enough.'

'He's already dead.' Freddy's movements were slowing down, his arms tiring from the ferocity of his attack. His voice was devoid of emotion, as distant as mine. Like mother, like son. 'But I have to make sure.'

Freddy grabbed the knife from Kayden's limp hand and stabbed him in the chin, working it from side to side, dislocating his jaws as he wrenched it brutally.

I brought my hands to my face, reflex telling me to cover my eyes, but my fingers spread as though of their own volition. Too much was happening too fast and it hurt, and I wanted to run, and I wanted to stare, and I wanted to get involved, and I wanted to be dead.

Freddy pried the blade free and lacerated Kayden's cheeks, and then brought the blade up in both hands and threw his whole body down, sinking the knife into Kayden's chest and holding it there, pressing his face down near the mess he'd made.

'Feel that, you fucking freak? Feel *that*? Do you? Do you fucking feel it?'

He twisted the blade around and around and around, staring as though in fascination at what he was doing. I did the same: watching far too enthralled as Freddy opened his mouth in a wolfish grin and then bit down on Kayden's lip, or what remained of it. At first I thought I was hallucinating, remnants of Paisley's drug gripping me.

But no – he gnawed and then spit soaked strips of flesh at Kayden's face.

'Freddy,' I whispered. 'You have to stop. You have to...'

My voice caught and I realised I was crying. I wasn't sure when I'd started, but my throat felt tight, choked. The fractured part of me collapsed into the actual and then *I* collapsed, my legs giving out.

I fell onto my side and gazed at the sickening show Freddy was performing.

I brought my knees to my chest and hugged them, weeping, pathetically and purposelessly because that's what I'd always been. I saw it now, clearer than I ever could before.

Pathetic. Purposeless. My whole life leading here, to this hate and pain and hell. My whole life leading to my punishment. Punishment for letting my boy go. Punishment for not fighting hard enough.

Mum was moving, her legs passing by me, an efficient shuffle. Maybe she was going into the garden: her escape, a way to pretend none of this was happening.

'I'm going to call the police,' she announced in a strangely official tone. 'Freddy, did you hear me? I'm going to call the police.'

Why was she *asking* him?

Because she was scared he was going to do the same to her. He was going to hurt her, lacerate her, misshape her. Her own grandson. She was scared of her own grandson.

'Fine.' Freddy was working the knife deep into Kayden's eye socket, staring with a sick grimace on his face. 'That's fine. Whatever.'

I glanced up to find Mum staring at me with her cheeks glimmering with tears. We met eyes for a moment, and I read the mess of emotion: the guilt and the regret and the pain and the apology.

The bitch. The fucking evil bitch.

She could've warned me about Kayden. But she didn't.

She'd lied to me for years and now she stared as though we were going to embrace and it would heal all I'd learned, all that had happened.

Mum left the room and I lay my cheek against the floor, thinking strangely about how soft it was, how clean it smelt. It was much cleaner than what Freddy was doing, than the butchery on the end of his blade. He picked it up and studied it like a curious boy in science class, and finally I closed my eyes against it all.

But it didn't help.

Paisley took shape in the darkness of my eyelids, a wet wide smile on her face, the sound of Freddy's mutilation becoming the harsh tenor of her voice. 'I told you I'd win, you stupid girl. I *always* win.'

58

Six months and the pain had not faded. The violence of Freddy's attack was a vivid, hateful kaleidoscope in my mind, each time I closed my eyes, a curtain of crimson pulling shut and locking me into the past.

I smelt the stink of Kayden's death in every meal: the blood, the shit, the sweat. I heard the *squelch* of the knife in muddy shoes across grass. The flicker of a passing bird became Freddy surging across the room, tackling him, brutalising him.

I'd moved out of Weston, quit FCA, and I was living in a nearby village and working in a shop. I'd turned myself into an automaton, focusing only on basic physical things. Stocking shelves, serving customers – with a fabricated smile if I could muster it – walking home, collapsing and staring at the ceiling. Writing had been impossible after everything which had happened. The words, which had once flowed so easily, refused to appear. Or perhaps that was an excuse; perhaps I knew I didn't deserve the outlet, not after what I'd done.

But I couldn't keep this stowed away inside anymore. As I watched the sun glitter against Theo's gorgeous London office, I knew it was time Theo knew the truth. I couldn't live in stasis.

This feeling was working its way inside of me, like a voice screaming.

Do something, do something now. You can't be passive forever.

Freddy had received seventeen years for his use of excessive force against Kayden. Whenever I thought about him, my lover, my son... whatever I thought, it was a pitiable fate. He'd saved my life and now he would rot away the best years of his life. He had become a shell of a person. I hated him: hated what we did, rather. And I hated myself. I never wanted to see him again, and yet I needed to hold him and tell him it would work out in the end.

Kayden and Paisley had stolen my right to ever feel normal again. Each time I bought a coffee, stood in line at the supermarket, I expected legions of people to turn and point their fingers at me.

'Son-fucker! Son-fucker! She fucked her son!'

Kayden was dead. What about his sick mother?

I wasn't at all happy with letting her live unpunished. But I wasn't sure I was capable either: of what I'd have to do to make this right.

Theo's graphic design office sat across the car park, with a fancy calligraphy-style logo affixed to the spot next to the door. When a sleek silver BMW pulled up and the boy from my visions, my past stepped out, a shiver ran through me. I placed my hand over my mouth and watched as this tall handsome man – as sleek as his car, sleeker – walked on confident legs toward the front door.

I stepped from my place under a tree, raising my voice. 'Wait.'

He stopped, turned. His hair was cut neatly, and he was wearing a shirt and chinos and shiny shoes. He looked like a different species to me.

'*Ellie?*' He stepped forward slowly. 'What are you doing here?'

It was midday. He was returning from lunch. The last thing he had expected – if that grim twist to his lips was any indication – was to see me.

'I took the earliest train I could.' My voice sounded distant, ghostly.

It was as though, reflected in my first love's eyes, I could realise how pathetic I truly seemed. And right then, as we gazed at each other, I vowed to do something about it. I vowed to *do something*, full fucking stop.

'Why?'

We stopped inches from each other, so close I could smell his expensive cologne, musky, a scent from a different world. 'Because I needed to speak to you about our son.'

He gritted his teeth. For a moment he looked like Kayden, feral and ready to attack. 'Why would you drag that back up?'

'You've done a fine job ignoring it–'

'No,' he said flatly.

'No?'

'I won't let this happen. You can't show up at my doorstep decades after it's all said and done, and start... start throwing *accusations* around. It's not like I'm the only one who tried to forget it. You've never once tried to reach out to me.'

'Because I couldn't face it. But I have to. I can't run anymore.'

He glanced at the office door, glanced back to me. His fingers twitched as though he wanted to check his watch. I'd expected him to ask me inside, to show me a shred of kindness. But it was clear he wished I could go away.

Fine. We'd do it here.

'Face what? That happened a million years ago. We agreed to forget about it.'

'Did you know I blocked it out? Did you know I had a mental breakdown?'

'Ellie, why are you doing this now?'

'Because I fucked our son, and he's in prison for killing my husband.'

He looked at me for a long time, as though waiting for a punchline. I returned his gaze steadily. It was the first time I'd spoken that truth aloud since that evil night.

'I don't understand.'

'I'll explain it all. And then I'm gone, out of your life, forever.'

'I don't understand,' he said with more force, a shiver in his voice. 'You *fucked* our son?'

Again he looked at the door. I was naïve for ever thinking he would want to see me.

With a sigh, I explained it all right there, lowering my voice when more cars pulled up and people began to walk into Theo's office and the adjacent buildings, returning from their lunch breaks. We drifted over to the tree where I'd waited, as I told him about Kayden and Paisley and Freddy, our dear Freddy with his wicked smile and his goofy singing voice and that optimistic, unbreakable twinkle in his eyes.

Theo had tears in his eyes when I was done, but they weren't falling. They made his eyes shimmer but it was like they refused to slide down his cheeks, as though he wouldn't let them.

'Why the fuck are you telling me any of this?'

'Because he's your son.'

He spun on me, waving his hand through the air. 'Ellie, I loved you. I really did. But that was a long, long time ago. That was *centuries* ago. Do you understand? It was at least five lives ago. I've had serious relationships since then. I've made a career for myself. I've put that craziness behind me. And you come and – and – tell me *this*...'

Finally he let out a croak, reeling away as though looking at me would make him cry. He stood with his back to me, roughly pawing at his cheeks. 'You have to go.'

I flinched. I hadn't expected him to hold me, to console me, but it still hurt.

'Theo...'

'This is nothing to do with me. That's why I came here. That's why I've never returned to Weston. That sick shit, that sick twisted shit, none of it is my business. That boy, that poor boy...' He swallowed audibly.

'His name is Freddy.' My voice rose jaggedly, my chest cramping as I realised how truly alone I was. 'You can at least say his name.'

'*That poor boy...*' He spun back to me. His eyes were dry now, bloodshot but dry. 'He has nothing to do with me, with my life. I have a girlfriend, Ellie. We've been together for three years. I'm going to ask her to marry me. The last thing I need – *we* need – is to get involved in any of this.'

'But aren't you glad you know the truth?'

'Glad? *Glad?*'

'That wasn't the right word.'

'Yeah, no shit.' He ran a hand through his hair, reminding me of the hundreds of times he'd done it when we were kids. 'Is there anything else? Maybe a secret uncle whose dick you sucked?'

I gasped. 'Theo! That isn't fair–'

He ducked his head and paced toward his office. I watched him go, wondering what I should do. But I'd told him. That was the reason I'd come up here. What else was left? I could chase him, beg him to care: beg him to hold me, to tell me it wasn't my fault.

But Theo had locked away the past, the same way I had before it all came crashing down. The only difference was Theo had *chosen* to lock it up, and he would keep choosing it, no matter what I told him.

Turning, I walked on unsteady legs toward the road, toward my bus stop, ready to begin the journey home.

I was sitting on the train, my forehead resting against the cool glass, when my phone vibrated from my pocket. The train was almost back in Weston and it was raining, bleak, a complete contrast to Theo's bright, sunny world.

I watched the drops sluice and dance across the glass as the train sped forward, wondering who was ringing me. It was probably Georgia, the only person I spoke to regularly these days. I hadn't spoken to Mum since I'd found out what she did to Kayden all those years ago.

Taking out my phone, I saw that it was Mum. She'd tried ringing me a few times a month since it happened, but I'd ignored her calls. I placed my phone in my lap and waited for the ringing to stop. There was a pause, and then my phone vibrated again, telling me she'd left a voicemail. She never normally did that.

'Ellie.' I squeezed my hand tight around the phone as I listened to the self-pitying quiver in her words, the threat of tears. 'I know...' A pause as she gathered herself, a you-can-do-this croak in her voice. It was always about her. 'There's something... There's another entry in my journal. One you haven't read yet. One that explains what really happened.'

59

I have decided to tear out this page. I did terrible things to that poor boy, and no amount of justification will ever make that acceptable.

And yet I find I cannot destroy these words.

Perhaps I'm a hypocrite. Perhaps I seek forgiveness even if I know it will forever be beyond my reach.

I have referred several times in these writings to the Other, which I believed to be my strongest, most lifelike hallucination. With every ounce of reason I possessed – which, admittedly, was not plentiful – I thought the overlarge woman with the reek of cigarettes and the serpentine smile on her face was not real.

But, as the weeks and months distanced me from that evil house and my evil deeds, the truth of the matter began to reveal itself. I say *reveal itself* because that is how I experienced it at the time: a series of doors opening inside of me, sometimes one by one and sometimes several at a time, showing me things to which I had been blind.

She had first seen me on my first night at the house, when I'd gazed out of the window, staring into darkness. At the time she said it was happenstance, but I suspect that was a lie. Paisley was – and is – a very large woman: not the sort to walk miles out of her way in a remote corner of the village without reason.

The next day, when I returned from replacing the clock, she struck. She was waiting for me. She'd followed me. And she...

Do not pity me, please.

But Paisley beat me terribly. She fell upon me like a wild animal and threw me to the floor. I was stunned by how efficiently she could move. It was like there was a beast lurking beneath the folds of her body, all sinew and mean intent.

Once she was done, she perched atop me, her fingernails clawing into the sides of my head, staring down with a delighted twist to her lips. 'We're going to have some fun, aren't we? *Aren't we?*'

I told her yes: whatever she needed so she would get away from me. But my affirmation only made her keener, and she reached into her pocket and took out a flask, the type my father used to keep in his breast pocket on weekends.

'Good girl,' she said, pulling off the cap with her teeth and forcing the contents down my throat.

I spluttered and coughed and thrashed beneath her, but there was no way to avoid swallowing it. To this day I do not know what was in her concoction, but I believe there must've been something of everything: stimulants to keep me manic, relaxants to make me pliable, amnesiacs to toy with my mind, to turn me into the plaything she desired.

Whatever it was, it made what happened next seem very far away. I cannot say Paisley forced herself upon me, for I was moaning, kissing her back, doing as she asked. But I was not present for any of it. I had become a brain-dead pet, mindlessly obedient, as this witch's elixir obliterated my reason.

Paisley would visit me most days with more of her poison, smiling at me with pretend kindness from my doorway. I later learned – from my parents, of all people – that those in the village thought we had become fast friends. They thought we did crosswords together and that she was helping me with my garden. Paisley, despite her degradations, was a gifted gardener. I believe this was how she procured many of the ingredients in my daily dose.

Then things began to fade and break apart, shimmer and become real and unreal, as I have already related. Except there are things I have left out.

Here is the truth of the matter.

Paisley led me into the woods the day I met Kayden, and she was behind the tree with me, whispering vicious things in my ear. 'Look at that fit young body, eh? Look at those muscles. And think about how he'll look when he's hanging there, when he's swinging back and forth... touch yourself, touch yourself. *Or I'll do it for you.*'

I didn't want *her* to touch me, and so I did it.

(None of this makes it okay. Remember that. I am guilty. Remember that.)

Though I behaved as though Paisley was not there – for I truly believed she wasn't – she must have directed Kayden to pretend. I also suspect she told him to lie to me and say he was eighteen. Or perhaps I did imagine that part. In any case, Kayden was not on her drugs – as far as I can remember – and he certainly wasn't schizophrenic. She must've been forcing him too.

She did something else, before this meeting. This kills me to write about.

She brought me to her house and made me sit outside the window, telling me if I moved she was going to command her demons to tear me to pieces. I honestly believed her; by then she was the Other, my private tormentor.

Peering through the window, I watched as Paisley sneaked into Kayden's room. Delaney was away for work, which suited her fine. And Paisley did... she did what she did, and I watched, and later I ascribed these images to my mind-reading ability.

There were times when Kayden came to me by himself, and that was when we would hold each other. That was when we would talk of the future. I'm not sure how genuine any of this was, on either side. I'm not sure if he truly cared for me.

Whenever Paisley was present, the talk would become vicious and – as she termed it – the *games* would begin.

She loved her games. The things I have already detailed – the multifarious sufferings we would inflict upon Kayden – we did together. And, furthermore, Paisley would often do them to me when we were alone.

Looking back, I can only wish I ran. I can only wish I called the police. I can only wish I *did something*, instead of being so passive, instead of allowing myself to be used.

I saw her once in the months after the events I have related here. My parents had visited the cottage – in the hopes of finally fulfilling their dreams of renovation – and, of course, Paisley had happened by. She was probably making sure I hadn't said anything.

Paisley, turning on her convincing side, managed to persuade my parents to give her my phone number. She said she'd had it before but lost it.

Paisley rang me and asked to meet.

I knew the truth by then. And I had moved beyond my pathetic terror. I was angry.

She had picked the worst possible time to ask for a meeting, for I was in a place to which I'd never return: a land of righteous, unflinching rage, without the guilt and trauma that would later be heaped upon me.

I pretended to remember nothing about what had happened, went along with her *little game* when she played nice. She must've thought I had blocked it out when I smiled and wrapped my arms around her. I suggested we take a walk down the beach, and I lured her to the far end, where it was quiet in late autumn.

Then I fell upon her and struck her in the face, the chest, stunned by how weak and helpless she seemed. Without her drugs in my body, with my anger boiling me up, I felt powerful.

I threw her to the ground and began to kick her in the stomach.

I stopped only when she began to beg, writhing on the ground, her face slick with more blood than I had ever seen, even during our torment of her son.

'Please, please,' she wailed, clawing at my shoe. 'No more.'

Not killing her right then was a mistake. But I do not have it in me to take a person's life. She was hardly a person at all, but I couldn't do it. I stepped away.

'If I ever see you again, you're fucking dead.'

She rose to her feet slowly, wincing and wheezing, and for a second – half a breath – she smiled. But then the smile was gone, and she kept blubbering. 'You won't. I swear you won't. You'll never see me again.'

That was the moment: the smile. She was plotting her revenge.

Against me, against my future child, against Kayden, against the world, driven by the corruption inside of her.

And never mind we'd never done anything to her before she

unleashed her terror upon us. Never mind we would've been happy if we'd never met her.

Paisley doesn't care. She is the closest thing to a true demon I have ever met. She inflicts pain for the sake of pain. If there is such a thing as true evil, its name is Paisley Hunter.

60

I stared down at the page, my hands shaking, the paper shaking: the words distorting as tears brimmed in my eyes and burned down my cheeks. A whole six months she'd let us live as enemies. She'd let me believe she'd done that evil stuff to Kayden by herself. Half a year of hating her.

'Why didn't you tell me this at the start? Why did you tear these pages out?'

She sighed and turned to the window. 'Because I still did those things. I still... Oh, God, I still hurt that poor boy. All my life I've had to live with that guilt–'

'I don't care. I deserved to know the whole truth. Especially after what happened. With Kayden. With Freddy.'

Saying my son's name hurt. I rubbed at my cheeks, pushing the tears and the pain away, leaning forward and staring hard at my mother. 'So all that babbling in the other journal entries – all those hints, all that crap about the Other – Paisley was there the whole time, orchestrating it?'

Finally she looked at me. Her face was drained. She must've looked like this when she so easily fell under Paisley's spell. Not just her spell: her potions, her *drugs*. 'Yes, she was. But that doesn't make me innocent. Because I still did it.'

'You've kept this secret so you can keep beating yourself up.'

'I don't deserve forgiveness.'

I slammed my fist on the table, surprising her, surprising myself. 'Who said I was going to forgive you? Lying to me, pretending not to know Kayden. And then lying about *this*, on top of everything else? Jesus Christ, Mum... Jesus Christ.'

We were silent for a time, the rain pattering against the glass, reminding me of the times we'd sit here and read together. In my teenage years, on one of her good days – before Theo left and tore my mind apart – we would sit and listen to the rain and disappear into our own private worlds. But I'd never understood just how private Mum's truly was.

'So you attacked her. You beat her up. On the beach.'

She nodded. 'Yes.'

'But then, when they came back into your life, you let it happen. You didn't fight. You didn't warn me. You disappeared into the garden and you let it happen.'

Folding her arms across herself, she said, 'Yes.'

'Well, surely you can see that makes no sense. Where did your fight go?'

I could've asked myself the same question. I'd been dormant this past half year, paralysed, barely a person at all. Working in the shop, disappearing into my small room, pretending the world didn't exist. I'd left Paisley alone because what good would it do, to confront her, to try and make her feel guilty when she was clearly incapable of that?

But this changed everything. She'd used everybody: my son, my mother, *me*. She'd used us all and she was getting away with it. By being allowed to live, she was getting away with it.

Mum stared and stared at me, as though she didn't understand my question.

'Why didn't you fight, like you did before?' I snapped.

'Because I was scared.' She blinked, a single tear sliding down her cheek. Thunder cracked in the distance. 'Paisley had Kayden on her side, and Kayden was so fierce, so terrifying. And he was... I couldn't bring myself to hurt him more than I already had.'

'So you let him hurt me instead.'

'I didn't know he was hurting you.'

I laughed bitterly. 'No, of course not. You thought this psychopath and her warped son were here to make our lives better.'

'If you're searching for the logic in the mind of a schizophrenic, Eleanor, you're looking in the wrong place.'

I stood, waving the hateful pages at her. 'I don't accept that. And I don't think you believe it either. You can't use your illness as an excuse for any of this. You weren't suffering from psychosis when Kayden returned. You weren't suffering in the years after I... I gave birth to Freddy.'

I swallowed a painful lump, thinking of the boy I hadn't visited: would never visit. Locked up for a crime he'd committed only to save what we'd had, even if it had turned out to be grotesque and wrong.

'So stop fucking blaming your illness for everything. You could've told me about this at *any* time.' My voice rose to a near scream. 'It's not your *illness*, Mum. It was never your illness. It was you, you narcissist, always thinking about yourself. Never thinking about me.'

'Ellie–'

'I would've helped you, if you'd fucking told me. I would've helped you work through this.'

'There is no working through something like this.'

'Maybe you're right.' I let the pages fall, suddenly flooded with purpose. For the first time in six months, I knew what I had to do. 'I love you, Mum. You need to hear that. Despite everything, I'll always love you.'

'That sounds ominous.' She rose to her feet, walking around the table. 'Ellie, what are you going to do?'

I strode away from her, my fists clenched, pushing past the numbness and the self-hate and the fucking *stasis*. I was done letting the world happen *to* me instead of correcting things myself.

'Ellie,' she called after me, as I walked quickly through the house, silently saying goodbye to the thousands of memories which sprung up from every shadow. I was no longer crying as I pulled open the front door. 'Ellie! What are you going to do?'

Perhaps she sensed something. Perhaps she knew this was the end.

What else did I have left?

I refused to let Paisley win. There was only one way out of this.

Pausing, I glanced at my mother, with her silver hair cascading down her back, with her lined and beautiful face, with her fingernails darkened with the care of her garden. I stared at her and I loved her, and I hated her, and I knew she would try to stop me if I told her the truth.

'The right thing, Mum,' I whispered, hoping I was strong enough, hoping I had it in me. 'I'm going to do the right thing.'

I turned and walked into the rain.

EPILOGUE

Paisley Hunter handed twenty grams of good home-grown weed to the teenage boy and offered him a smile. She knew she sickened him, and this knowledge sent a tingle through her body, but especially to that warm place deep in her belly that had lit up ever since she was a girl: the first time she poured boiling water into an ants' nest, crushed a spider with her thumb, grabbed the neighbourhood kitty's tail and gave a sharp *yank*.

'Thank you,' the bright-cheeked lad said. He had freckles all over his face. His skin was shiny and tight and alluring.

'See you next time,' she purred, wondering if she still had it in her to go a few rounds.

She watched him leave, his long lean legs far too gangly for his body, not like her Kayden had been. So strong as a teenager, so full of life.

Lighting a cigarette, she returned to the living room and dropped into her armchair. She took a deep inhale and let her head fall back, closing her eyes as the nicotine rushed pleasantly around her body and the past rushed just as pleasingly around her mind.

She'd had a good run of it, hadn't she?

She'd played her games, so many games, and all of them had brought her great pleasure.

No, it wasn't the search for pleasure – she mused as she took another blessed inhale – it was the staving-off of boredom. All her life, boredom had been her greatest enemy.

Perhaps it had led her down some unconventional paths, what with how she'd toyed with little Kayden. But he had learned to appreciate it in his older years, to moan with her, to rock with her.

Her hand snaked down her body, toward that tingly hot spot, as she thought about the first time he'd started to moan.

Like this, Mummy? Like this?

She let her hand drop, opening her eyes with a sigh. Kayden was dead and the fun had stopped, and she was simply existing, watching her shows and tending to her plants and smoking her cigarettes. The whole world had abandoned her, leaving her to sink into this hole of boredom.

But there was simply no way she could top what she'd already achieved.

Lottie had been a gift sent from heaven. The first time Paisley had spied her sitting in the upper window of that run-down piece of shit estate, she'd felt something new, something exciting. It was the look in the mad young woman's eyes: the frantic, defenceless look. She was practically screaming, *Please use me any way you desire.*

Paisley had taken her opportunity, because she would've been a fool not to. Using special herbs from her garden – her beautifully useful garden – she had turned Lottie to her will. It had been much more exciting having another involved in the game, a new aspect to the pleasure, and doubly so because Lottie was a complete nutter.

Paisley giggled under her breath as she remembered it all:

the long greasy hair and the grimy fingernails and all that pacing, all that muttering. She finished her cigarette and lit another, laughing again, longer this time.

Oh, God, that tingly spot was properly humming now. But there was nobody around to fix it.

Fucking Kayden, the idiot. Why did he have to get himself killed?

That had been Paisley's greatest game: biding her time after that beating Lottie gave her, letting the plan take shape in her mind. Once that mad bitch had laid hands on Paisley, there was no way she could let it go, especially because Paisley had been forced to grovel and beg her to stop. Humiliating, absolutely fucking humiliating that was.

But some instinct told her to wait, some finely-tuned hunter instinct. That was the only good thing her husband had ever given her, the name Hunter. That and the fresh-faced lad who'd brought her so much joy.

Years she waited, nurturing Kayden, telling him that Lottie had abandoned him, she hated him, she'd broken her promise. Paisley had known about their plan to abscond together, because Kayden had told her. He told her everything.

She'd made sure of that in his early years. He would fear her above all. She would be his owner. He was her pet. She didn't phrase it in those terms to him, of course. She cradled him and stroked his teary cheeks. She comforted him in the ways he grew to relish.

But deep in her heart, she knew what her son was: a tool.

She always knew that, when he came of age, she would find a way to use him. And she did. She found so, so many ways. He would bring women back to the house and they would engage in threesomes, Kayden telling the poor drugged-up lasses that Paisley was his girlfriend.

Sometimes they would give her this look, this proper slutty

look, like they thought they were better than her. That's when she would give them the *special* dose, the one that would knock them out cold, and together she and her son would make patterns on their limp gorgeous bodies.

Kayden helped her tend the garden, expand her dealing network beyond their corner of the world. He had his flings, his dalliances, but he always came home to Mummy in the end.

'Mummy knows best,' Paisley whispered through a cloud of smoke. 'Mummy *always* knows best.'

She had to talk to herself now, after Kayden's death. She really did miss him: his smile and his reassuring hand atop hers, and how he always told her she was pretty, the most beautiful woman alive. They both knew it wasn't true, but he had been such a loyal, well-trained thing.

She did *not* miss her husband, and was glad when the cancer struck him. That was yet another sign she was doing the right thing. God had taken him instead of her, leaving her and Kayden to do as they wished. Paisley had been planning to give him some special herbs anyway. Fate had simply sped up the process.

Delaney had always been so fucking uppity, giving her subtle jabs about her weight, about the attention she lavished on their – no, *her* – son. If it wasn't for Delaney, perhaps her original plan would've taken shape. Perhaps she and Kayden would've killed Lottie and buried her in the woods, next to the tree where she and Kayden first met.

But that beating Lottie gave her...

It stayed with her for a long time, the disgrace of lying on her back on the beach, the struggle of standing up. The *pride* in Lottie's eyes. Paisley had never taken a beating like that before. Not from her parents – and they'd given her plenty – not from her husband, and *certainly* not from a psychotic cunt like Lottie.

Her first instinct had been to fight back – Lottie had used a cheap surprise tactic, sucker-punching her, and would be easy work in a proper scrap – but then another idea occurred to her. And she'd smiled.

Paisley was a patient animal, oh yes, and she kept watch on Lottie.

A plan was taking shape in her mind, a beautiful and precious thing, but she wasn't sure if it would ever come to fruition. There were too many variables. And yet she knew that, if and when it did happen, she would be able to die a happy woman. This was to be her magnum opus.

She sent Kayden down to Weston many times over the years, tracking Lottie's progress, until Ellie came into the world. And that was it: another sign.

Paisley knew better than anybody how deep a mother's love went. She would use it against Lottie. Honestly, she'd expected Lottie to *do* something when Kayden appeared in her daughter's life, but she didn't.

She'd retreated into her sad shell. Paisley had enjoyed the marriage while it lasted, having Kayden send her videos of their games.

'How long do I have to stay married to her?' the lad would grumble from time to time. 'It's a lot, Mum, what I do to her. It takes a lot from me.'

He could be weak sometimes.

'Until that bitch tries to get involved,' she'd snapped. 'Until she's forced to tell her daughter the truth.'

Paisley knew how much that would hurt Lottie, cracking open that aspect of herself, revealing her secret past with Kayden. But she never had.

So Paisley had thought of another plan, an escalation that would make it worth it.

'Next time she starts blubbering about leaving you, let her. Let her and come home to me.'

Oh, what a year she and Kayden had shared, what a romance they'd ignited!

They'd spent long afternoons in the living room together, Kayden cradling her close to his chest, his hands pawing across her skin. He'd had his episodes, as usual: about how wrong this was, about how he wanted to stop, blah-blah-blah. But it was easy to shut him up. All she had to do was threaten to take her own life and *poof*, away his worries went.

Paisley Hunter *always* won.

Then it was time for Kayden to die and come back to life, and that had gone so well, so much better than she'd–

The doorbell cut through her thoughts. She groaned and glanced at the window through a haze of smoke, at the sun against the curtains. Sometimes the more nervous lads forgot they had to knock on the window. Then she could call over to them, telling them the door was unlocked, saving her a trip.

Hauling herself to her feet, she went to the door, ready to give the dolt a piece of her mind. Young boys were insufferably stupid sometimes. That's why they needed an older woman to put them right.

She opened the door, but there was nobody there. Nobody at the end of the lane. She gritted her teeth and leaned down to spit, and then she saw the note, resting on the step, weighted down with a stone.

What nonsense was this now?

She picked it up with some effort, cursing the idiot who'd left it for not wedging it in the letter box.

The handwriting was jagged, as though the writer had been angry.

You lose.

Suddenly there was a hand on her shoulder, a cold kiss of metal at her throat.

'Any last words?' Ellie hissed in her ear. She'd recognise that voice anywhere, the superior slut who always thought she was better than everybody else.

Paisley froze, rage boiling in her. Ellie, fucking *Ellie*. 'Do you really expect me to believe you're capable of this, girl? You're a scared, pathetic thing, just like your mother. Put the knife down and...'

Ellie cut deeply in a powerful fluid motion, and Paisley Hunter collapsed forward as the blood gushed down her body. She tried to roll over but the pain bit too sharply in her throat. She tried again, gurgled as she failed to curse. If she could roll onto her back, she might be able to see her favourite photo of Kayden, the one she purposefully kept in the entranceway so it would greet her when she arrived home.

Closing her eyes, she pictured it instead. It was his first day of school and he looked so happy, so proud, with that indomitable smirk on his face. His eyes were bright. He was ready to make his mark on the world. And they had; together, they'd done amazing and beautiful things.

As the final flickers of life left her, Paisley Hunter smiled softly. She was going to be with her son.

THE END

ACKNOWLEDGEMENTS

As always, I'd like to thank everybody at Bloodhound. Without them, I wouldn't be living my dream as a published author. Tara, Hannah, Fred, Betsy – thank you so much for your endless support. I'd like to give a special thanks to Ian, my editor, for his wonderful suggestions during the first wave of editing; Ian, you helped make this a far better and more robust story.

Writing can be a lonely endeavour, so I count myself lucky to have friends like Patricia Dixon, Heather Fitt, and Keri Beevis. You three are always there if I ever need to discuss anything, writing or personal and everything in between. I'll never tire of making fun of you... or having you three make fun of me. It's a true honour to feel like, no matter what, I've got you backing me up.

I'd love to list all the people I've met through Facebook bookish discussions this past year, but it's impossible; there are too many wonderful people. But for everybody who shares a meme, comments on one of my posts, puts up with my incessant marketing, shares stories about their families and their pets and their hopes and their dreams, I thank you. You make this digital workplace so much more exciting.

As always, I'd like to thank my friends and family. Mum and Dad, my brothers Ben and Jake, Marshall and Joey and Kane and James, you make this life so much more fun and interesting. I'd also like to thank the Weston Rollers group, for giving me a way to escape the pressure of work for a few hours every week.

Most importantly, I'd like to thank my wife, Krystle. Without her I never would've written a single word. Krystle, I love you and Gizmo and Loki so much, and I'll never stop being grateful for your support.

A final thanks is owed to you, the reader, for getting this far. It means the world to me to know that you finished my twisted and macabre story. I hope you were able to take something from it, and that it didn't take too much from you.

A NOTE FROM THE PUBLISHER

Thank you for reading this book. If you enjoyed it please do consider leaving a review on Amazon to help others find it too.

We hate typos. All of our books have been rigorously edited and proofread, but sometimes mistakes do slip through. If you have spotted a typo, please do let us know and we can get it amended within hours.

info@bloodhoundbooks.com

Printed in Great Britain
by Amazon